RISING
Assets

A MAVERICK MONTANA NOVEL

Rising
Assets

A Maverick Montana novel

Rebecca Zanetti

Entangled Publishing, LLC
2614 South Timberline Road
Suite 109
Fort Collins, CO 80525
Visit our website at www.entangledpublishing.com.

Brazen is an imprint of Entangled Publishing, LLC. For more information on our titles, visit www.brazenbooks.com.

Edited by Liz Pelletier
Cover design by Heather Howland

Manufactured in the United States of America

First Edition March 2014

For Stephanie Cornell West, the most loyal person I know. I love you.

Chapter One

"She can't be working here. No way." Colton Freeze leaned forward in his chair and slid his nearly empty beer on the battered wooden table. A jukebox belted out Garth Brooks, peanut shells lined the floor, and longnecks took residence on almost every table in the bar. Unfortunately, the sense of home failed to relax him.

"I'm only telling you what Mrs. Nelson said at the bank." His friend, Hawk, turned toward the long, oak bar. "If she is working here, I wish she'd show up so I can go home to bed."

"Soon." Colton shook his head. "There is no way Melanie works at the coffee place in the morning, her ranch all day, and Adam's bar at night." And she hadn't bothered to tell him. He'd been out of town finishing his master's degree and then securities degree, and nobody had thought to tell him his best friend was working herself to death? Fear slammed him between the eyes, nearly bringing on a migraine. He shoved the sensation away.

"I didn't know, or I would've called." Hawk gazed thoughtfully across the smoky room, his odd green eyes narrowed.

"You've only been home a day." Colt frowned. He cocked his head as the bartender called out with a friendly, "Hi, Mel."

Damn it. She *was* working in the bar. Colton steeled his shoulders and schooled his face into a pleasant expression. If he yelled at her right off the bat, she wouldn't talk to him.

He needed to speak with her. While they'd grown a part a little bit during their teenage years, when they'd moved on into the world, they'd kept in touch as he attended school. After her grandfather had died two years ago, they'd reconnected, and Colton had made sure to call, text, and email while he studied.

After a short time, he couldn't sleep without talking to her and sharing his day. Maybe he should've been home instead of pursuing knowledge.

As his best friend, she was needed. Plus his gut churned that she hadn't shared her problems with him. "Where in the world is she?" he muttered.

She stepped out from behind the bar, and he straightened in his chair. "What the hell?"

Hawk emitted a slow whistle. "Wow."

Yeah, wow. Melanie's customary outfit of faded jeans, scuffed boots, and a working T-shirt was absent for the night. "Adam must have made her wear the outfit." Son of a bitch. He'd kill the bar owner.

Hawk leaned forward, elbows on the table. "She looks good."

She looked better than good, and shock sprang Colt's cock into action. A tight tank top showed off perfect breasts, while a skirt curved along her butt to stop a couple of inches away. Long, lean legs led down to high-heeled boots. She was a wet dream come true.

Melanie wobbled a full tray of drinks to deliver to a table of rowdy farmers.

"Maybe the medical bills from her grandpop's fight with cancer added up, and she needed the extra money?" Hawk rolled his shoulder and finished his beer.

Colton exhaled but couldn't look away from the sexy brunette. Sexy? Jesus. It was just the shock of the new look. She was still Mel, still his best friend. "So now I need to worry about both of you. What the hell?"

Hawk sighed. "Tell me you didn't ask me out for a beer my first night home to lecture me."

Colton turned toward his oldest friend. Lines of exhaustion fanned out from Hawk's eyes, and a dark purple bruise mottled his left cheekbone. He was usually battered when he returned home from active duty, but this time a hardness had entered Hawk's eyes. Now wasn't the moment to bug him, however. Colton shrugged. "Nope. Just wanted to catch up. I'll push you tomorrow on leaving the SEALs."

"Fair enough." Hawk took a deep swallow of his beer as his gaze remained on Melanie. "I'm glad you called. It appears as if things might get interesting tonight."

Doubtful. Colton turned his attention back to the woman who hadn't trusted him enough to let him know she was in trouble. Something in his chest ached, and he shoved the irritant aside with anger. While he was known for a slow-to-burn temper, especially in comparison with his two older brothers, when he exploded, it was legendary.

But there'd be no temper tonight. First, he had to figure

out what the hell was going on, and then he had to solve the issue. Logically and with a good plan. So when Mel glanced his way, he lifted his empty glass.

She nodded and hitched around full tables to reach him. "Why did you cut your hair?" Her face was pale as she tried to tug her skirt down.

He knew she wouldn't be comfortable half nude in public. "When the hell did you start waitressing in a fucking bar?" The words slipped out before he could stop them.

"Smooth," Hawk muttered into his beer.

Melanie arched a delicate eyebrow and released the bottom of the skirt. "Last I checked, my grandfather was dead and you weren't my keeper. Do you want another beer or not?" The tray hitched against her hip—a hip that wasn't nearly as curvy as it had been the previous year. She'd lost weight.

Even so, he wanted to grab that hip and… "What time do you get off?" he asked.

A dimple twinkled in her cheek. "It depends who I take home with me."

He couldn't help but grin back. "You are such a big talker."

"I know." She shoved curly brown hair away from her face. Hair wild and free. "Why are you asking? Think you'll need a ride home?"

"I'm taking you home, and we're talking about your three jobs." He tried to smooth his voice into charming mode, but the order emerged with bite.

"The last time you tried to boss me around, I hit you in the face and you cried for an hour." She nodded at a guy waving for a drink from a table on the other side of the dance floor.

Colton threw the guy a glare. "I did not cry."

"Did too," Hawk whispered.

Colton shot a look at his buddy before focusing back on Mel. He'd been seven years old, and she'd almost broken his nose. "My eyes watered from the punch. That wasn't crying." They'd been having the argument for nearly two decades, and the woman never let up. "You've cried on my shoulder many a time."

She reached for his glass. "That's because men are assholes, and you have great shoulders."

Every boy or man who'd ever hurt her had ended up bashed and bloody afterward because either he or Hawk had made sure of it. "You're right on both counts. Which begs the question, if you're in trouble, why aren't you crying on my shoulder now?"

Sadness filtered through her deep eyes. "You're my friend, not my knight. It's time I stood on my own two feet."

But he wanted to be her knight, because if anybody deserved protection, it was Melanie. "I'm mad at you."

"I know." She smacked his shoulder. "You'll get over it. You always do."

Was it his imagination, or did regret tinge her words? He tilted his head and studied her.

She smiled at Hawk. "I'm glad you're home. You staying this time?"

Hawk lifted a shoulder. "We'll see. It's nice to be among friends, I can tell you that."

Mel nodded and fingered Colton's short hair, returning her attention to him. "Why did you cut it?" she asked again.

That one touch slid down his spine and sparked his

balls on fire. What in the hellfire was wrong with him? He shifted his weight. "I thought it was time for a more mature look since I'm taking over at the office." Of course, last time he'd grappled at the gym, his opponent had gotten a good hold on Colton's hair. At that point, a clipping had become inevitable.

Mel smiled. "You do look all grown up, Colt Freeze."

He'd love to show her just how grown up. At the odd thought, he mentally shook himself. Friend zone. Definite friend zone. That was it. "Part of being a grown-up is asking for help."

She rolled her eyes. "I'll be back with another beer." Turning on a too-high heel, she sauntered toward the back corner.

Colt's gaze dropped to her ass. The flimsy skirt hugged her flesh in a way that heated his blood. While Mel was small, she had always been curvy. More than once, he'd wondered.

For years he'd gone for wild girls…fun, crazy, and not looking for forever. During his life, he'd avoided anything but friendship with Melanie, who was a keeper. A good girl, smart as hell, and kindhearted.

Hawk cleared his throat.

"What?" Colton asked.

"You're looking at Mel's butt." Hawk set down his beer. "How long have I been out of town, anyway? Has something changed?"

Colton shoved down irritation. "No. Besides, what's wrong with Mel's butt?"

"Nothing. In the world of butts, it's phenomenal." Hawk leaned to get a better view. "Just the right amount of muscle and softness. In fact—"

"Shut up." Colton jabbed his friend in the arm. Hard. "Stop looking at her ass."

Hawk chuckled. "If you're finally going to make a move, let me know. I have a hundred bucks entered in the town pool."

Colton's ears began to burn. "Town pool?"

"Yep. The exact date you and Melanie finally make a go of it." Hawk pushed back his chair. "Now that you're home, get ready for some meddling."

"Mel and I are just friends." He'd kill himself if he ever hurt her. In fact, he'd beaten the shit out of her first boyfriend in high school because the prick had cheated on her. So the fact that she had an ass that made Colton's hands itch to take a hold of, was something he'd ignore. Again.

"I may stay home for a while, because this is going to be fun." Hawk stood. "Mind if I head out? I need sleep."

"No problem." Colton shook his head. Hawk did need sleep if he was thinking Colton and Mel could be anything more than friends. The three of them needed each other, and things had to stay the same. "I'll see you at your southern pasture at dawn. The order of twine finally came in earlier."

"Can't wait." Hawk turned and headed out of the bar, seemingly oblivious to the several pairs of female eyes tracking his progress.

A voluptuous pair of breasts crossed Colton's vision before a woman plunked down in Hawk's vacated seat. "Well, if it isn't Colton Freeze," June Daniels said before sliding her almost empty wineglass onto the table.

"Hi, June." Colton forced his gaze to her heavily made up eyes and away from the twins being shoved up by a bra worth twice whatever the woman had paid for it. "How are you?"

June pouted out red lips. "Almost empty."

"We'll have to get you another." Colton slid a polite smile on his face. While he may be single and definitely horny, he was far from stupid. The four times divorced cougar leaning toward him represented a complication he neither needed nor wanted. Talk about not fitting into his plans. "Are you out by yourself tonight?"

"Yes." She clasped her hands on the table and shoved her breasts together in a move as old as time. "How about you since Hawk took off?"

"I'm waiting until Melanie is off shift." It wasn't the first time he'd used his friendship with Mel as an excuse, and it probably wouldn't be the last.

June sniffed. "Why? She's still dating the oldest Milton son from Billings, right? The banker?"

Colton lifted a shoulder. If Mel was still dating the banker, it was the longest relationship she'd ever had. The idea shot a hard rock into his gut, one he'd have to figure out later. His unease was probably due to the fact that any banker wearing three-piece suits and allowing his woman to work three jobs wasn't good enough for Melanie. Though using the word *allow* around her would end in a broken nose. Colton smiled at the thought.

Melanie slid a beer in front of him and leaned over to pour wine into June's glass.

June narrowed hard eyes. "How did you know what kind of wine I want?"

Melanie recorked the bottle. "You're drinking red. *This* is our red."

Colton bit back a grin. Adam's wasn't known for a fine

wine selection, but beer was another matter. "Did you bring me a nice beer?" He glanced closer at the thick brew. "Looks hearty."

"Suck it up and try the new beer, wimp." Mel nudged his shoulder.

June leaned closer to Colt. "We were discussing you and Brian Milton."

Melanie eyed Colton. "Is that a fact?"

The tone of voice held warning and had the unfortunate result of zipping straight to Colton's groin. He felt like a randy teenager all of a sudden, and enough was enough. "I wasn't." If all else failed, throw the cougar under the bus. "June brought up Milton."

"Why?" Melanie turned her formidable focus onto June.

"Curiosity." June's caps sparkled even in the dim light. "You've been dating for quite a while. Is it serious?"

"It's personal." Melanie dropped a couple of beer napkins on the table. "I have a ride home, Colton."

"Yeah. Me." He took his drink and gave her his hardest look—one that wouldn't faze her a bit. "Either agree, or there's gonna be a hell of a scene in the parking lot when I toss your ass in my truck."

Sparks flashed in Melanie's eyes. She leaned in, and the scent of lilacs and woman almost dropped him to his knees. "Threaten me again, Freeze, and I'll make you cry for hours."

He'd never been able to refuse a challenge, so he turned his head until their lips hovered centimeters apart, his gaze piercing hers. "Sounds like a date."

Chapter Two

Melanie stretched her calves in the front seat of Colton's truck and bit back a wince as his headlights illuminated a downed fence on her property. Then another—both nearly covered by snow.

"What the hell?" he asked.

"I've been busy."

He glanced her way, a new tension cascading off him. "What about your crew?"

"Let them go. No money to pay them, but I do contract with Hawk's crew whenever I need help on a case-by-case basis." Her feet pounded in pain, and goose bumps covered her bare arms. God, she hated working in the bar outfit with a passion rivaling a Freeze temper.

"Is that why you're working three jobs?" he asked quietly.

"Yes, and don't even think about offering me money." Her neck prickled. Sure, he was rich. She didn't want his money—she never had, and she sure as heck didn't want to discuss her reasons for needing money. Not now, anyway.

"How's the ranch doing?" Colton asked.

"Great. I have fifty head in the south pasture, the Angus bulls in the north pasture, and all of my foals to the west." She loved ranching and had never considered another career. Montana was home, and she had no problem mucking out stalls when necessary.

"Crops?" Colton asked, his genius mind obviously doing calculations.

"Winter wheat, barley, and Camelina." The oil seed crop was used in biofuel, and it had been Colt's recommendation she plant it last year. "The money will come in, and I'm not worried." Right.

He rubbed his chin, settling back in the seat. "How about a loan?" In the moonlight, the interesting multicolors of his hair still shone, even though the mass no longer touched his shoulders. It seemed like the finest genes from both his Native American and Irish ancestry had combined into hair color women paid a fortune for.

"I don't want a loan." She studied his angled profile. Hard and sharp, his even features showed a rugged toughness he'd lacked as a cute teenager. Now he was all man.

A pang hit her that someday he'd settle down. Finally become one woman's man. Lucky wench. The man planned his entire life down to exactness. His future wife was probably some PTA president with as many college degrees as he had.

Melanie hadn't had time for college, and she liked her boots muddy. Dirty boots didn't belong at PTA meetings.

His muscled shoulders rolled, and he kept his gaze focused out the window. "Working three jobs is too hard and too stressful." Colt stopped the truck in front of the porch she'd painted the week before.

Thank goodness something looked fresh.

Distant or close by, he'd always been overprotective, and she could take care of herself. Time was short, and she needed money, not protection. "Stop worrying." She slid from the truck. "Thanks for the ride home. I'll talk to you tomorrow." Slamming the door shut, she loped up the steps and unlocked the front door.

The engine cut behind her. A door slammed, and heavy boot steps echoed behind her. "I can't help but worry. You're going to work yourself to death."

There was no alternative. God, she needed to get out of the skimpy clothes. She hurried inside, kicked out of the heels, and dropped her purse on the sofa table.

"Why do I get the feeling you're not telling me everything?" He remained on the porch.

Sighing, she allowed her shoulders to drop as she turned to face him. The man had excellent instincts. "I'm not telling you everything."

Colton stilled. "Excuse me?" he asked softly.

She swallowed. The tone of voice was something new. "Some parts of my life are private."

He blinked. "No they're not. If you're in trouble, Hawk and I are here. The three of us."

Exactly. This was a problem the three of them couldn't solve. It's not like she'd ask either one of them to impregnate her. "I know, but I'm on my own with this one."

"There is no *on your own*, damn it. It's not how we work." Colton vibrated with a very rare display of temper.

Irritation crawled up her throat. "Listen, Colt. I know

you're used to meddling family members and the security that comes with that, but back off. I'm alone, and I need to figure this out by myself." It was a low blow, considering he'd always felt badly about her lack of family and his abundance of it, but she had to get him off the topic of money and her need for it.

"You're kidding me. I can't believe you said that." His chin lowered.

She'd known him her entire life and had seen him truly angry twice. Maybe three times. The man had an incredibly long fuse, but if it blew, everyone scattered.

As he stood in the doorway, blue eyes blazing, there was no question as to his fury.

She lifted her chin and casually moved toward the nearest chair, suddenly feeling vulnerable in the tight outfit that revealed way too much. "I don't need your help."

"Sit down." The order held bite and rumbled in a deep tone she'd never heard. Yeah, she may have poked a slumbering bear. Her butt hit the cushion even before her mind clicked into gear. Instant anger swelled through her at how quickly her body had followed his order. She shot to her feet.

"Too late." Long strides propelled him so close she could feel his heat. "Stick with your instincts and not with that stubborn mind."

She turned slightly to outmaneuver him. "I don't take orders from you, Colton Freeze."

He mimicked her motion and stepped into her space. "If you're not smart enough to take care of yourself, you damn well *do* take orders from me."

Anger and a well-earned note for self-preservation

battled for dominance inside her. She took a step back. "Get out of my house."

He mirrored her step. "No." Crimson angled across his high cheekbones, enhancing the dangerous hollows beneath them. As a kid, he had been adorable. As a teenager, handsome. As a fully grown, tough, battle-scarred man, he was all predatory male.

One she was smart enough to back away from, even as her nipples sprang to attention from his intense gaze. Oh, this couldn't happen. *Down nipples. Down.* Several steps later, her butt hit the wall.

A second later, they stood toe to toe. His palms flattened against the cedar logs, caging her. "We're about to come to an understanding here, Melanie Murphy Alana Jacoby. Got it?"

Heated air filled her lungs with delicious tingles. She breathed out slowly, trying to control herself.

He'd been her best friend for decades. She knew how to appease him, how to make him laugh. The right words were there and would smooth everything over. For two seconds, she considered saying them. But she was past that. He'd come into her home, he'd ordered her around, and now he wanted things his way.

Not a chance.

So she said the one thing guaranteed to push him over the edge. "Fuck you, Colt—"

His mouth was on hers before she finished saying his name. Heat and power slammed from the kiss, and her mind swam.

Fire lashed through her so quickly her knees weakened. Her nipples scraped his chest, and lava consumed her. Her eyes fluttered shut, and she fell into the storm created by a man much more dangerous than she'd known.

She kissed him back, her body alive, her mind shutting down.

There was nothing but the whirlwind of impossible need cascading around them, through her, into her, beyond her.

The kiss was hard, angry, and more passionate than she could've dreamed.

Many times they'd come close to kissing, but one of them had always backed away. With a grin, or a joke, they'd escaped ever taking the chance. The one thing Melanie knew for sure was if Colton ever kissed her, if he ever showed her that side of him, there'd be no turning back. Ever.

As he released her mouth to pin her with a dark gaze, there was no question he knew it, too.

Determination filtered through his eyes, and his jaw firmed. Something new and intriguing fluttered alive in her abdomen. Satisfaction lifted his lips as her eyes widened.

Holy crap. Colton Freeze didn't want to turn back.

Chapter Three

After a damn restless night, Colt kicked the post into place, his stomach empty, wind slapping his cheeks and scattering snow across his boots. "The weather is supposed to warm up in March. Where's the damn sun?"

Hawk rubbed a well-worn glove across his forehead. "It's only five in the morning. Give the day a chance."

"Whatever," Colton muttered.

His brothers glanced up from tying off twine around a fence post.

"What's eating you?" Quinn asked. As the sheriff in town, Quinn often stepped in before anybody threw a punch. Well, unless it was Quinn aiming the fist.

"Nothin'." Colton shook his head. One sleepless night didn't mean a damn thing.

His oldest brother, Jake, leaned into the back of a battered truck to grab a thermos. "What's up, Colt? Is your detailed plan for this week off track?" Jake shared a look of amusement with Quinn.

"I don't plan everything," Colton said.

"Do too," his brothers muttered right back.

"Whatever. I'm just chomping at the bit to get into the office later." Not true—not true at all. His mind still spun from the disastrous kiss the previous night. What the hell had he been thinking? Kissing Melanie was not in any plan.

Even worse, his body didn't regret it nearly as much as his mind. In fact, his body wanted to march right back to Melanie's and finish what they'd started.

His body could shut the hell up. "How's Sophie?" he asked Jake.

"Great." Jake grinned like he always did when talking about his spunky wife. "She's starting to show, and having some fun shopping for maternity clothes."

"I think this time you're having a girl," Quinn said, reaching for another fence post.

"Either would be great, but I do think it's another boy," Jake countered. "Just a gut feeling."

"Twins," Colton said with a grin. It was nice seeing both of his older brothers married and happy, although he had no intention of joining them anytime soon. Jake had married an artist and already had a baby boy, and Quinn had married an art gallery owner, and their wives had become instant friends.

Hawk scratched his head. "What is she, about five months along?"

"About that," Jake said. "This pregnancy was a complete surprise considering Nathan is only a year old. We could find out the sex but decided it'd be fun to wait and see. My daughter is hoping for a girl this time."

Little Leila was from Jake's first marriage, which had left him a widower. It was wonderful seeing both Jake and Leila happy with Sophie in their lives now.

Leila would be a great big sister no matter what. At eight years old, the sweetheart was more fun than imaginable. "Tell her to be ready after dinner for our movie night," Colton said. He liked to take his niece to the movies every time a new Disney came out.

"She already picked out her outfit." Jake grinned. "She won't tell me what you two have planned for the St. Patrick's Day float."

Colt reached for a hammer. The family always entered a float in the Mineral Lake St. Paddy's Day parade, and this year, he and Leila had volunteered to create the design. "Let's just say it involves vampires and werewolves that don't sparkle."

"Sounds good." Quinn stretched his back. "Let us know when we need to show up and pound nails."

"It's a plan." Jake cut a look toward Hawk, his gaze intense. Colton nodded imperceptibly.

"All right." Jake threw a hammer that clanked in the back of the truck. "Quinn and I will head over to the northern pasture and check on the fences before going into town. I have an early meeting with some clients." As a lawyer, Jake often had early meetings.

Quinn slowly gazed at Colton and then Hawk. "Good idea. See you two later." Sliding into the front of the Ford, he waited for Jake to jump into the passenger seat.

As the brothers drove down the bumpy field, Hawk turned toward Colton. "That was subtle."

"Huh?" Colton asked, stretching his neck.

"I figured all three of you would discuss my options with me." Hawk wiped grime off his forehead.

Colton shrugged. "We didn't want to gang up on you." But they would if they had to. Hawk was family, and when family needed help, you jumped in. "I can call them back if you wish."

"No thanks," Hawk said. "Get the prompting over with."

"When do you need to decide on re-upping?" Colton asked.

Hawk sighed, his green eyes narrowing. "A month. I leave on another mission any day, and then I have a month to decide."

"Want to talk about the mission?" Colt asked quietly.

"Can't." Hawk kicked a post into better alignment.

Figured. Colt's gut ached whenever he thought about Hawk's time as a sniper in the service, but he understood they couldn't talk about it. "I need another partner in my business, and I want it to be you."

"You don't need another partner, and I doubt you have a partner to start with." Hawk grabbed the post with both hands and twisted the base deeper into the earth.

"I want you and Mel as partners. It'd be more fun, and you have capital." Colton reached for more twine.

"You're richer than dirt and don't need my capital."

"Come on. You've given your time, and you've done a lot of good. It's eating you alive, and that won't work. We always talked about owning a series of fighting gyms, and now is the time." Colt set his jaw. He'd enjoyed MMA fighting while in college and wanted to bring fighting and different martial arts classes to gyms throughout Montana.

"Don't you think you'll be busy with running Lodge-

Freeze Enterprises?" Hawk asked.

"Sure, but I want this business for the three of us." He'd never planned on only working as the CEO for the family companies, and even as young kids, he, Hawk, and Mel had planned to work together. Of course, as teenagers, he and Hawk had thoughts of owning a Hooters-type bar until Melanie had vetoed the idea.

As adults, they had different priorities than just fun. Colt's current one included getting his oldest friend home in one piece. "You look tired." Obsessed. Dangerous. Haunted.

"I'm fine." Hawk rolled his shoulders and glanced down the row of repaired fences that protected cattle and didn't delineate any division between their ranch lands. Since his mother had died, they'd worked the ranches as one. "One more mission—something I need to take care of, and I'm out. I promise."

Colt paused. "The mission sounds personal."

"Missions are always somewhat personal." Hawk's face lost expression in a way that pissed Colton off.

He hid his irritation. "So, about our partnership?"

"You're the financial genius." Hawk finally smiled. "What's the plan, anyway?"

"I thought we'd start with a gym in Mineral Lake and one in Billings…and expand from those locations. Teach martial arts, some fitness classes, and self-defense. Should be fun, and it's not like we lack training." Colt finished with the last tie-down. "What do you think?"

Hawk straightened his back and looked toward the snow-covered mountains to the north. He rubbed his chin. Finally, he turned toward Colton, dark eyes somber. "After this month, I'm in."

Relief whipped through Colton so quickly he turned away to throw tools in the back of the remaining truck to hide his expression.

"So how about now you tell me what's bugging you?" Hawk loped toward the vehicle.

"I kissed Melanie last night." Colt had never kept a secret from Hawk, and he had no intention of starting now.

Hawk halted and swiveled around. "Holy shit."

That pretty much summed it up.

"Did she kiss you back?" Hawk shoved his hat further up his head.

Colton paused. Hell yeah, she'd kissed him back. With fire, with tongue, she'd pretty much blown his world. "Yes."

Hawk rubbed his chin. "Well, it was either that or punch you in the face. What does this mean?"

Heat roared through Colt's chest. "Nothing. It means nothing. The kiss was a temporary moment of craziness. I hadn't seen her in too long, she wore that dress, and I was, ah, pissed." Right? That was it.

"Um, okay." Hawk stepped into the passenger's side of the truck and waited for Colton to get in. "But why? You guys are great together."

"The three of us are good together." Colton slid into his seat and ignited the engine. Where one went, the other two showed up. The security of their friendship had made for a good childhood for them all, and they couldn't leave Hawk out. He'd lost everybody but them.

"I'm not into threesomes."

Colton snorted. "Did you just make a joke?" His buddy had been way too serious for much too long.

"I'm funny," Hawk said.

Hawk was many things, but funny wasn't one of them. Laconic. Serious. Deadly.

Colton nodded, steering the truck around potholes. "You are hilarious."

"Thanks." Hawk wiped dirt off his forehead. "The three of us are great friends, but you and Mel have always had something…separate. Something just for you."

Colton jerked his head. Had they abandoned Hawk?

Hawk cut him a look. "It's a good thing, and I never felt left out."

Was he telling the truth? The friendship with Mel and Colt had been all Hawk could hold on to for so many years. Hawk had never known his father, and he'd lost his mother as a teenager. Colton would never exclude him. "Mel and I are good friends." No male-female stuff. Well, until last night. "We know everything about each other. No intrigue, no surprises, nothing to take us further." Plus, he wasn't ready for forever, and he'd just hurt her.

Then he'd have to kick his own ass.

"Hmmm." Hawk pressed a button on the radio. "We all didn't hang out as much as teenagers. Ever wonder why?"

"We were busy with sports and dating. But we still hung out a lot."

Hawk shrugged. "Maybe you two didn't want to watch each other date other people."

That was just silly. "Whatever."

"Aren't you tired of bubble-heads?" Hawk asked.

Colt skirted a sprawling hole and headed for the nearest ranch road. "Bubble-heads? Shawna was an anthropologist with a doctorate."

"Yeah, but she was dumb." Hawk shrugged and then

winced as the soundtrack for *Grease* belted out. "Perhaps book smart, but the woman couldn't hold a conversation to save her life."

Colt thought back to the voluptuous blonde. "We didn't talk a lot."

Hawk snorted. "Exactly."

Like Hawk talked very much. This conversation included more words than Hawk usually used in a week. Colton shoved a rough hand through his hair as the music continued. "Apparently Melanie was in the truck. Why does she still like those soundtracks, anyway?"

Hawk shrugged. "I don't know. But *Grease* was the first movie the three of us watched together. Remember? We snuck the VCR tape from her grandpop's movie stash right after she moved here."

That was right. Mel had only been four, a chubby little girl with sad eyes. Her parents had died in a small plane crash, and her grandpop had instantly brought her home to raise.

Colton had taken one look at her and decided they were going to be friends for life. The idea that she still loved the music because of him and Hawk was a sweet one. "I remember."

Hawk rolled down his window. "Mel's all grown up. How do you feel about her marrying somebody else and building a life?"

A possessive edge cut through Colt and brought him up short. "Marry?"

"Sure. She's a sweetie, and hot to boot. She'll get married and settle down."

Colton frowned, not liking the panic heating his blood.

"Humph."

"I figured you hadn't thought it out." Hawk leaned an elbow on the window. "You might want to do so."

Colton's mind spun. "I'll give it some thought. For now, what do you think about Melanie working to oversee the construction of the gyms as her part of the start-up costs?"

"Great idea." Hawk peered through the windshield as the sun finally appeared.

"She doesn't have experience," Colt said.

"So?"

Colton nodded. "She'll look out for our interests, and the contractors I'll hire will have experience."

Hawk nodded solemnly. "I'd feel better with Melanie keeping an eye on things."

Now that was a friend. "Me too. Um, I think something's going on money-wise with her."

"More than the ranch and her grandpop's bills?"

"Yes." Colton rubbed his eye. Melanie wouldn't spend money frivolously or just lose it. Something had to be going on.

"Ask her."

"I did."

"Then give her some space. She'll ask for help when she needs it." Hawk wiped condensation off the window.

"Maybe." Colton shook his head. He wasn't great at giving space—never had been.

Hawk chuckled. "When are you breaking ground on your new house?"

Colton shrugged. He'd been planning to build a house on the other side of the ranch and was now living in one of the small cabins skirting the west side. It suited him as he got settled. "Not until we get the gyms going." His plan made sense, and he'd stick with it.

"Do you think Mel will agree to supervise the construction?"

"Yes." Now all Colton had to do was convince Mel she was needed, and she truly was. He needed her to stay healthy, relax, and make some money…and her watching over the construction would be an added bonus. "Wish me luck."

"Luck," Hawk drawled.

Colton ignored the amusement in his friend's voice. He'd convince Melanie to oversee the construction, and they'd go back to being buddies like always.

How hard could it be?

• • •

Melanie bussed coffee cups from another table, her mind still spinning. She'd kissed Colton. He'd kissed her.

Boy, had he kissed her.

"Hi, Melanie," a chipper voice said.

Melanie turned to see Colt's young niece standing behind her. "Hi, Leila. I just cleared a table for you."

Leila shook out her long hair. "I got a haircut. See?"

Melanie smiled and shared a look with Leila's grandmother, Loni. "You look beautiful, sweetheart," she said.

"Thanks." Leila slipped into the nearest seat. "Uncle Colt is taking me to the movies tonight. Do you wanna go?"

Heat flushed through Mel until her cheeks ached. "I would, but I have plans." Somewhat true. Since she had the night off, she planned on cleaning her house and catching up on laundry. Even watching a movie if she had time to rent one.

"You gotta date?" Leila asked.

"Nope." Melanie straightened her back, her vertebra cracking. "What can I get you two?"

Loni reached out to brush a motherly hand across Melanie's forehead. "You look flushed. Feeling okay?"

Sure. Except Loni's youngest son had kissed Melanie senseless the night before. She forced a grin to the woman who'd stepped in years ago and taken Mel bra shopping when her grandfather had needed assistance. At that point, noticing how lonely the teenaged girl was, Loni had checked in often. "I'm fine. Just bustling around," Mel said.

Loni's black eyes sparkled in her pretty face, her Native American heritage creating an interesting combination of smooth angles. "Good. I've been worried about you working so much."

Not for the first time, Melanie wondered about her own mother. What would it be like to have such concern for every hour of every day? She cleared her throat. "Hey, Loni. I wanted to say thanks."

Loni lifted her head, dark eyes wise. "For what?"

Melanie shook her head. "For being there for me… always. I needed you, and you were there."

Loni patted her hand. "Of course I was there…we're family."

Yet they weren't. Not really. "I know." Melanie smoothed down Leila's dark hair. The eight-year-old had inherited her grandmother's delicate build and thick hair.

Leila grinned. "When are we gonna have another *Grease* marathon at your place?"

Melanie laughed. "Any time, and you know it. This time we can sing along loudly because I bought the karaoke system we found on the internet. Now, what can I get you two?"

The outside door clanged, and the air changed. Not in a perceptible way, but with a way that raised the hair on Melanie's arm. She knew who'd walked in before she turned around.

Her heart dropped to her knees.

Colton walked in dressed in a full blue suit with striped power tie.

She gulped, her hands clutching on the rag. They'd known each other their entire lives, and she'd never seen him in a full suit. Even for school dances, he'd looked more cowboy than savant.

Today he looked like exactly what he'd become: one of the most influential and powerful financial geniuses in the Pacific Northwest. His hair was ruffled, enhancing the perfect angles of his handsome face. A powerful build filled out a suit costing more than her beat-up pickup.

His ideal mate definitely wore designer heels and not scuffed cowboy boots. The chick probably even spoke French. Or Italian. Or some fancy language that educated people knew.

His gaze warmed when it raked her. "Morning, Mel."

Shivers cascaded through her stomach. "Mornin'." Why the hell was she looking at him so differently? One kiss, one that was a colossal mistake, shouldn't change anything.

The kiss *hadn't* changed anything, damn it.

He nodded at Kurt behind the counter. "*To go* today, thanks."

Kurt tipped his bushy head and ducked to steam some milk.

Colton pressed a kiss to his mom's cheek and reached to drag Leila up for a hug. "How's my favorite girl today? Ready for our date?"

Leila smacked him noisily on the nose. "Maybe."

Colt's eyebrows lifted. "Maybe?"

Leila pouted. "I don't know."

Mel cleared her throat, and when Colton glanced her way, she tugged on her hair.

Colt grinned and snuggled his niece closer. "But you have such a new pretty haircut. We have to go out and show it off."

Leila gasped in delight. "You noticed."

"Of course—you look all grown up." He settled her back in her seat and mouthed a *thank you* to Mel.

A pang shot through Melanie. Someday Colton would have kids and a life of his own, and she'd be relegated to the status of old friend. A surprising hurt spiraled through her.

"You okay?" Colton asked.

"Sure." Melanie smiled as Kurt sauntered over to hand Colton his drink.

"Good." Colton slid cash to Kurt and kept his focus on Melanie. "Because I was wondering if you'd mind driving into Billings to the office today—perhaps for lunch? I have a business proposition for you."

"What a lovely idea," Loni said with a smile.

Melanie narrowed her gaze. Loni and Leila being in the coffee shop simultaneously with Colton was no accident. The manipulative man had arranged the situation. "Oh, I—"

"I already know you have the night off, and I sent one

of our crews to take care of your downed fences today." The smile Colton flashed was filled full of dare. "So I think you have time."

Irritation slivered across her skin, but she couldn't very well let him have it in front of his mother. "But I—"

"Oh," Loni exclaimed, digging into her purse. "Since you're going into Billings, would you do me a huge favor and return this brooch to Jillison's jewelry store? I would go, but I'm not up to par today, and today is the last day I can return the piece for full value."

Melanie faltered as she accepted the high-end bag and took a good look at Loni.

She looked great. Fantastic, even. Bright eyes, good color, sweet smile.

Even so, there was no way Melanie could refuse. "Of course. I'm happy to help." She'd planned to go into the city at the end of the week for an appointment, so maybe she could change the day, anyway. She shot Colton a look promising retribution, and his smile widened.

"It's a lunch date, then." Amusement twinkled in his blue eyes. "I will see you ladies later."

Melanie forced a smile as he loped from the coffee shop. She had just been expertly maneuvered by the best. And… had he said *date*?

Chapter Four

Colt shoved a stack of manila file folders to the side of his desk, his mind on emerging markets. He'd invested the family holdings heavily in a start-up green science company out of Seattle, and six months ago, he'd been convinced it was a good idea. It had fit his grand plan perfectly.

Now he wasn't so sure, although the owner was a buddy from college. Had Colton invested too much? He'd been so confident—maybe to the point of cockiness?

Colton had still been in school, although he'd unofficially taken over for his father as CEO of the company long ago. Now his dad took care of the main ranch and enjoyed semi-retirement with Loni.

Colton pressed both hands against the heavy wooden desk. How many times had he played around it while his father had worked deals sitting in the very chair Colton sat in? How many school reports had he finished in the office, always enjoying the dealing and financial aspects?

His dad and Jake and Quinn's dad had been business partners long ago. In fact, the desk had originally belonged to the boys' father. He'd died in a snowmobile accident when the boys were young, and after a couple of years, Tom and Loni had fallen in love, gotten married, and had two more kids—Colton and Dawn.

They'd combined the ranches and family business into one. One that rested on Colton's shoulders. For now. In a couple of months, Dawn would graduate with yet another degree, this one in business. She planned on studying overseas for one more year, and then she was coming on board. Their little sister loved school.

A blond head poked inside his door. "Mr. Freeze? Your sisters-in-law are here to see you."

Colton glanced up at his new secretary with a grin. They had to be about the same age, and the formality had to go. "Thanks, Anne. And please...call me Colton. The *mister* makes me feel old and decrepit."

Anne smiled. "Fair enough. I'll send them in." She disappeared from view.

Sophie, Jake's wife, was the first through the door, all energy, even in her fifth month of pregnancy. "Hey, bro. We were in town shopping, and I thought I'd drag you to lunch since Juliet has to get back to the art gallery." Her wispy blond hair feathered around a cute, pixie face.

Juliet followed gracefully behind Sophie, her red hair curling around her shoulders. She'd married Quinn last year, and her calm nature made the sheriff relax in a way he hadn't in eons. She glanced around the stately office. "Are you going to decorate more to your tastes?"

Colton frowned and looked around at the paintings

that had adorned the walls for decades. "Probably not. Although…I'm thinking of moving headquarters to Mineral Lake."

Sophie clapped her hands together. "Great idea."

Juliet pursed her lips. "With the internet and so many people working from home, there's no reason you'd have to drive to the city. When are you thinking about moving?"

He shrugged. "I wanted to talk to the family first, but I was thinking within the year."

"That's a great plan." Sophie bounced up on the balls of her feet. "Now come feed a starving pregnant lady, would you?"

He grinned and crossed around the desk. "Melanie should be here in a few moments, so why don't we wait for her?" Then he could butter Mel up with good food before hitting her with his business proposal.

Sophie's eyebrows lifted. "Mel's coming into town?"

"Yes."

"Oh." Sophie slipped an arm through Juliet's. "Well, now. In that case, I'll just grab something on the way home." She started dragging Juliet from the office. "I wouldn't want to impose."

Colton hustled to follow them to the doorway. "You're not imposing." Not that Sophie had any problem inserting herself in any situation if she deemed it appropriate. "Mel should be here any minute."

"No, no, no." Sophie waved as they reached the outside door.

Juliet halted their progress and looked down several inches at Sophie. "You have a day this week in the town pool, don't you?"

Sophie snorted. "Of course not."

Juliet glanced toward Colt, her eyes sparkling. "I think we should accompany them to lunch."

"Nah." Sophie tugged harder. "I know you have sometime in next month for their get-together date."

Juliet's eyes widened. "I most certainly do not."

Sophie laughed. "When you lie, you sound like a countess."

Colton shot them both a hard stare. "Please tell me you're not in on some Maverick County bet that involves me."

"Nope," they said in unison.

Sophie won the struggle and yanked open the door. "The bet only involves the town of Mineral Lake and not the whole county. Bye, Colt. I'll talk to you later." The door closed behind them.

He had to find out more about this stupid town pool. Colton cut a look at Anne. "That was interesting."

Anne smiled, all professional. "Your sister-in-law has a lot of energy."

Now that was the truth. Scratching his head, Colton turned back toward the stacks of work on his desk. "When Melanie Jacoby gets here, please send her in. Thanks."

The entire town of Mineral Lake needed to get the heck out of his business.

• • •

Melanie wiped damp palms along her faded jeans. She should've worn a dress, but jeans were her normal look. Yet as she entered the stately brick building that housed Lodge-

Freeze Enterprises, she wished for a different style.

One that fit with a gazillionaire like Colton.

Then she shook her head. Man. They'd been friends since preschool, and he knew everything about her. Well, almost. He didn't give one hoot how she dressed.

She pushed open the door and stopped short.

"Hi," said a gorgeous blonde from behind an antique desk.

Yeah. Melanie's biggest nightmare skirted the desk in a pretty pink suit, green eyes sparkling, hair perfectly styled. Colton's exact type, right down to the plus-sized boobs.

"You must be Melanie," the stunning woman said.

"Yes." She held out a hand to shake. The woman's manicure matched the smooth suit. "Nice to meet you."

"You too. I'm Anne, the office manager *slash* secretary *slash* receptionist." The woman gestured Melanie toward a plush chair in a stylish waiting room. "Colt said to send you right in, but he's on the phone with a broker from Taiwan — something about emerging markets — so how about I give you a heads-up when he's finished?" The smile was genuine and the tone gentle.

"Thanks." Melanie tried not to leave boot marks in the thick carpet as she crossed to take a seat. Next to Anne's style, Mel looked like a cousin from the freakin' boonies. From *that* branch of the family tree.

"I love your boots." Anne leaned over for a better look. "Where did you get them?"

Mel glanced down at the Lucchese hand-tooled boots. "My grandfather gave them to me for my birthday a few years back."

Anne smiled. "They're amazing."

Yeah, they were. Melanie smiled her thanks. What the heck? The perfect blonde who was lucky enough to work with Colt all day needed to be snotty or arrogant, not *nice*. Melanie wanted to dislike her. A lot. Instead, she was very much afraid she'd just made another friend.

The outer door opened and a miniature bundle of pure energy ran inside. "Mama!"

Anne stood, her eyes widening. "Tyler. What's going on?"

A robust woman followed through the doorway, a kid's backpack over one shoulder, a stack of haphazard papers in her hands. "I'm so sorry, Anne, but my daughter was in a car accident, and I need to go to Seattle. Immediately." The woman dropped the bag on Anne's desk and turned back to the door. "I'm so sorry."

Anne gulped. "It's okay. Let me know how your daughter is."

The woman left.

Anne swallowed, turning pale. Her lips faltered as she smiled. "So it's you and me today, baby."

Tyler smiled and nodded before zeroing in on Melanie. "I'm Tyler. I'm three."

Melanie grinned at the little cherub. He had his mom's green eyes and spiky, crazy blond hair. Pudgy cheeks showed a couple of dimples. "I'm Mel."

Colton's door opened and he stepped outside.

Anne hurried around the desk. "Mr. Freeze, I'm so sorry, but my day care lady had an emergency." She brushed hair from her face. "I know this isn't a place for kids—"

"Tyler," Colton said with a grin. "Dude. How's it going?"

Tyler launched himself at Colt, who swung him up in a wide arc. "Good. I ate goldfish."

"Yum." Colton tucked the toddler more securely into his side. "Tell your mama to call me Colt, and tell her you can work here any day. Always."

The moment hit Melanie square in the abdomen. Colton was a natural with kids; in fact, he was a natural with this one.

Anne fluttered her hands. "It's just that—"

Colt rolled his eyes and set Tyler on the desk. "Stop sweating the small stuff, Anne. Kids have always run amuck in this office, and I wouldn't want it any other way."

The woman nodded, blinking rapidly. She obviously needed the job.

Melanie attempted a reassuring smile. "There's a spot in Colton's office where we carved our initials when we were seven. Over by the wooden file cabinet." Of course, it had been Tom's office at that time. And he'd decided to leave the initials in place, even through several repaintings of the office.

Anne grinned. "I saw those—there are three sets."

Hawk had been there, too.

Colton strode forward and slung a friendly arm around Mel's shoulders. "We're heading out to lunch. If you need to take a half day and go hang with Tyler, no worries. If you want to stay here and work together, no worries. So…no worries."

The last was said with a firm note that caused the oddest fluttering in Melanie's belly. And he wasn't even talking to her.

"Thank you," Anne said quietly.

"See ya later, Colt," Tyler called out.

"Bye, buddy." Colton all but propelled Melanie out of

the door and through the building. "I'm starving. Besides the latte earlier, I haven't had a thing to eat. Tell me you're hungry."

Melanie lifted a shoulder. "I could eat before we fight."

"We're not fighting." The firm tone returned.

Melanie glanced at his hard face. "Does anybody ever win a negotiation with you?" Those Taiwan businesspeople didn't stand a chance.

Colton's natural grin made him seem even more approachable, if that was possible. "Yeah. You, Hawk, Dawn, Leila...family always wins." He casually switched their positions on the sidewalk so he walked between her and the street. "Well, unless I'm right. Then I win."

"Are you ever wrong?" she asked, trying to bite back a smile.

"I'm sure it has happened." He opened the door to a quiet deli.

Mel nodded and chose a table near the window to sit. The quaint restaurant had checkered tablecloths on the tables and movie posters on the walls. "What's up with your receptionist? Cute kid." Hopefully Anne was married.

Melanie didn't want to analyze why that mattered to her. Not now.

"She's a single mom and is the best organizer I've ever seen." Colton glanced at the specials scrawled across a chalkboard.

"Anne is very pretty." Melanie studied the hand-printed menu.

"Huh?" Colton focused back on Melanie and shrugged. "I guess. But I need a good assistant, and she's excellent. I don't care what she looks like."

Right. "You're not blind, Freeze."

The bubble-gum-popping waitress showed up to take their orders.

Colton smiled, instantly sending the teenager into swoon-mode. "I'll have the roast beef on sourdough, and the lady will have turkey on whole wheat with extra pickles."

The teenager nodded and bopped away.

Melanie kicked Colton under the table. "Turkey isn't what I wanted."

He lifted an eyebrow and studied her. The seconds ticked by until she couldn't stand his gaze any longer. "Okay. Turkey may be what I wanted…this time. But you might've been wrong."

"This is a great sandwich place, and turkey is your favorite sandwich."

She lifted her chin. "You don't know me as well as you think."

"I know you kiss like a goddess."

She could only stare. Yep. That was Colton. If there was an issue, a problem, he charged head-on into it. No coyness, no subtlety, no hidden agenda. "I can't believe you said that," she finally choked out.

He took a sip from a sweating water glass. "I figured we should talk about the kiss."

"Why?" She shook her head, panic heating her lungs. She couldn't lose Colton as a friend, not now. Definitely not now. "We're friends. We slipped. It's over."

"I know." He rubbed his cut chin. "But, well, I liked kissing you. It felt—"

Right. It felt right. She nodded. "I know. But we've been best friends forever. I mean, *forever.*" He and Hawk were the certainties in her life. The limited stability she could claim.

Of course she was attracted to Colton—the guy was all hard angles and good nature. But he also had gone through women like toothbrushes for a long time…and she didn't want to be relegated to an old drawer in the bathroom.

Plus, his girlfriends were usually blond, beautiful, and buxom. Melanie didn't fit into any of those slots. The mere idea of Colton seeing her naked sprang hives over her chest.

The waitress slipped their baskets before them and hustled off to wait on a group of boys who'd just sat down.

Colton eyed his large sandwich. "Is it Milton? Are you serious?"

Melanie reached for a chip. No. She and Brian were more like buddies, but it was nice having somebody as a plus-one. "I don't know. We've been dating for a while, but I'm not sure where we stand." In fact, she probably would know more later after her doctor's appointment, but she didn't want to go into her problems with Colton. Yet.

"Okay." He took a bite of his food. "Remember when we talked about owning a business together as kids?"

She grinned. The boys had wanted to own a strip club, and she'd wanted a horse farm. "I do remember."

"Now's the time."

"No." She shook her head, shoving down hope. "I can't invest right now."

"I know. Hawk and I will bankroll the start-up costs, and your third will be in labor—overseeing the construction and the publicity of the first two martial arts gyms. One in Mineral Lake and the other in Billings."

She tapped her fingers on the table. "I appreciate the vote of confidence, but I don't need a handout."

He grinned, and at that point, she empathized with the

Taiwanese broker.

Leaning back, he sighed. "Listen. We need somebody on the front lines, and I'm too busy taking over the business, and Hawk will be overseeing the fighting. It would set his mind at ease to know you were looking after things."

Fire flushed through her. "Don't you dare use Hawk as an emotional point." She hated that he had to leave again for danger so far from home.

Colton shrugged. "I'm just telling you what he said. Plus, we'd have to pay somebody to oversee the construction, so we might as well pay you. We trust you, and now you don't have to work three jobs. Win-win."

"No." She shook her head. "You're not planning my life. Period."

He sobered. "Believe me, I'm not planning anybody's life right now."

She frowned, concern focusing her. "What's wrong?"

He shrugged, an odd vulnerability darkening his eyes. "Maybe nothing. I invested heavily in a business, and it may have been a mistake."

Colton Freeze making a financial mistake? Melanie raised both eyebrows. "Ouch. Can I help?"

"Yes." His upper lip quirked. "Please come on board to oversee the construction of my baby. I need somebody I can trust so I can concentrate on the other matter."

God. He was impossible. Talk about going for the jugular. Or heartstrings. But owning a business with Colt and Hawk had always been one of her dreams, and there had to be a way to make it happen. She would like to help him, and this might be fun. "If I do agree, then that's my buy-in. No salary."

"We need the salary because we already included the line item as a cost in the construction loan."

Oh, he had an answer for everything, didn't he? She bit her lip. "I wouldn't mind burning the outfit from Adam's bar."

"Now that would be a pity."

She focused on Colton. "Stop flirting with me."

"Can't help it. I know how you kiss." His tone rumbled guttural low.

She rolled her eyes. "I would love to call your bluff, Freeze."

"Not bluffing."

He wasn't. She knew him, and if she made a move, he'd meet her more than halfway. "Our friendship is the only stable thing I have right now. The only stable thing in Hawk's life. I'm not going to ruin it."

"Why haven't we ever gotten together?" Colt's brows drew down in the middle.

She kept herself from squirming on the chair. "By not sleeping with you, I remained in your life. Special." Which was the absolute truth.

He grimaced. "I'm not that bad."

"No, you're not." In fact, he was freakin' amazing. "But you've never wanted to get serious or settle down, and usually whoever you were dating did. So when it ended, you avoided them." If Colton ever avoided her, it would break her heart.

"I'd never avoid you."

"I never wanted to take the chance." Now she winced. "Plus, now we're too different."

"What?" His cheek creased. "We both own ranches and love it. How are we different?"

"You're loaded with a ton of degrees. I only took one class in college." She squirmed in her seat.

"Seriously?" His amusement fled. "Degrees are just degrees and have nothing to do with intelligence, work, money, or anything else." He shook his head.

"Said the guy with a bunch of degrees." She smiled. Sure, she was smart. But still.

"That's the dumbest thing I've ever heard. If you want a bunch of degrees, go get them. You're one of the smartest people I've ever met, and you thinking this is crazy."

"Maybe. Even so, I'm staying in the friend arena." Warmth flushed through her that he realized she was just as smart as he was…even without diplomas.

"Like I said, you're an intelligent woman." Even so, regret filled his eyes for the briefest of moments. Then his cell phone buzzed, and he glanced at the face, quickly returning the text. "Hawk's in town looking for us. He should be here in a minute."

In less than a minute, Hawk strode in, wearing flak and not cowboy boots.

Melanie's heart dropped. "You're heading out."

"Yes." Any peace or relaxation Hawk had earned while on leave had fled, leaving his face a hard, cold mask. "Just got my orders. Wanted to say good-bye."

Mel skirted the table to duck into a hug. "Be careful, and come home."

He hugged her back, longer than usual. "I will. You be safe, take care of Colton, and protect my business interests while I'm gone."

She leaned back to smile. "You planned this."

"Nope." A small smile flirted with his lips. "But I want everything in place when I get back. Please."

"Okay." There was no other answer she could give.

"I promise if you come back safely, I'll take care of the construction."

"Excellent." He released her and turned as Colton stood.

Never afraid to show emotion, they hugged, and a lump settled in Melanie's throat.

"Come back." Colton stepped away.

Hawk yanked an envelope from his back pocket. "Just in case." Long strides took him from the room.

Concern bracketed Colton's face as he watched his friend leave. Then, tucking the envelope in his pocket, he sat.

Melanie sat back down. "What's in the envelope?"

Colton shrugged. "He leaves one with me every time, and it feels like a bunch of letters. I'm assuming they're for us, probably my mom, and my sister. But I never look, just give it back when he gets home. Like I will this time."

Melanie stilled. "A letter for your sister Dawn?"

"They're good friends."

Dawn and Hawk were a lot more than friends, but now wasn't the time. So Melanie nodded and tried to smile. Why did it seem like things were changing? She glanced at the rest of her sandwich, no longer hungry.

She considered asking Colton to accompany her to the doctor's appointment later but quickly discarded the idea. There had to be some personal distance between them if they were going to remain friends and now business partners. Inviting the man to her appointment required an intimacy they didn't have and never would.

Something in her wanted that closeness with him.

For the first time, she wondered if their childhood friendship could last into adulthood when deep down, she was beginning to want more.

Chapter Five

Colton pushed back in his chair and surveyed his office. Dark paneling covered with landscape paintings of Montana, and more specifically, Maverick County. When he relocated, he'd take the same paintings.

They were home.

Quiet ticked around him since Anne and Tyler had gone out for a late lunch. God, he felt unsettled. Hawk was gone, Dawn was still at school, and now Melanie was dating a banker. One not good enough for her. Plus, the idea of her really falling in love with somebody else turned him cold. He needed her, damn it.

The idea that he needed her so much worried him. This didn't fit in with his life plan for the next few years.

His phone buzzed, and he smiled when he saw it was Sophie. "Hi, Soph. What's up?"

"Colton?" her voice emerged high and frantic. "I'm ten minutes out of town, and something's wrong."

"Whoa." He stood, already crossing his office. "Wrong with what? The car?"

"No," she whispered. "The baby. I can't find Jake, and I'm an hour from home and Doc Mooncaller. I don't know what to do."

Panic rushed through Colton to be immediately squashed. There wasn't time for panic if Sophie needed help. He calmed his voice into a soothing tone. "Where are you?" He loped into a run through the office and outside to his truck.

"I pulled over at the Exxon gas station outside of Billings." Tears filled her voice.

Colton started his truck and drove into the street. "Okay, Sophie. Here's the deal. You sit in the car, take deep breaths, and try to calm down. I'll be right there, and I'll take care of everything."

"Okay." She took an audible deep breath.

"Give me an idea of what's happening."

Her voice caught. "I had a bad twisty zing of pain, and now I'm spotting."

Shit. That couldn't be good. "Where's Jake today?" Colton asked, his mind calculating the best scenario.

"He's at the federal courthouse in Billings, but his phone is off, so he must be in court."

"Okay." Colton pulled onto the interstate. "I need to hang up for a second and make a couple of calls, and then I'll call you right back. Okay, sweetheart?"

"Okay." She sniffed.

He hung up and dialed one of his financial clients, the best gynecologist in Montana, and received quick reassurances that they'd see Sophie as soon as he got her there. Then he dialed the courthouse and was told that Mr. Lodge was in court.

"I'm sure, but I need you to get a message to him," Colton said to the curt woman on the phone.

"I'm sorry, but not while he's in court." Derision dripped from the woman's tone.

"Listen lady, we have a family emergency, and you need to fucking get my brother out of court. Now." Colt's rare temper began to compete with the panic sweeping him. "Believe me, while you don't want to face Jake's wrath, you *really* don't want to deal with me. Tell him to meet me at Rollings Women's Center. *Now*."

"Well," she huffed. "I'll see what I can do." She clicked off.

Colton fought a growl and took the exit for the gas station. He found Sophie sitting in her car, tears on her face, pure terror in her eyes. Instantly, he shot into calmness.

"Any more pain?" he asked casually as he helped her from the car.

"Um, no." Her face relaxed marginally. "But it's too early for the baby to arrive." Panic reasserted itself as the color slid from her cheeks.

"The baby is not coming." He lifted her into the truck. "This is a glitch, happens all the time." Shit. What the hell did he know about pregnant women and babies?

She grinned, her lips trembling. "Been studying the issue, have you?"

No, but he should've been. He shut her door and jogged around to jump in the driver's seat. "Sure. This is just fine, but we're going to see a doctor anyway. The best in the country."

"The entire country, huh?" Sophie's shoulders relaxed

even though her hands shook in her lap. "How fortunate that he lives in Montana."

"Where else would he live?" Colton fought for a reassuring tone as he pulled back onto the interstate, forcing himself to only drive a few miles over the speed limit. Okay, twenty.

He cleared his throat. "Did anything like this happen with your last pregnancy?"

"No."

He glanced over, not liking the dark circles under Sophie's eyes. She looked way too delicate and frightened. "This will be fine. Take another deep breath."

They arrived at the clinic in record time, and Sophie started to open her door.

"Wait." Colton jumped out and crossed around to lift her from the truck.

"I can walk, Colton."

"No." He hustled into the clinic and marched up to the receptionist. "Doctor Jordan is waiting for us."

The door flew open behind them, and Jake ran inside.

Oh, thank God. Colton turned and deposited Sophie in her husband's arms.

Jake snuggled her close. "Are you okay, Sunshine?"

A nurse opened a door by the receptionist and motioned them inside. "The doctor is waiting for you."

They disappeared after the nurse. Colton swallowed and walked over to sit, dropping his head in his shaking hands. What if he hadn't gotten there in time? Had he driven too quickly and hit too many potholes? What if—

He lifted his head and took several deep breaths. Enough. He'd just sit in the plastic chair and wait for the good news. It would be good news. He wanted to call Quinn or their dad but decided to wait until he heard something. Anything.

So he called the ranch and gave instructions for somebody to drive out and fetch Sophie's car.

Then he waited.

Alone in the waiting room, he watched as woman after woman, all in different phases of pregnancy, went in for an appointment and then left. Some were accompanied by men, some by other women.

Finally, Jake and Sophie exited the mysterious land of pregnant women.

Colton stood and schooled his face into calm lines. "Well?"

Sophie smiled, weariness in every line of her body. "I'm okay."

His butt hit the chair. Thank God.

She touched his shoulder. "Deep breaths, Colton."

He chuckled and stood to hug her. "That's excellent advice." Then for good measure, he hugged his older brother. "We're sure?"

"Yes." Jake clapped him on the back, black eyes still worried. His power tie was askew, and he'd removed his suit jacket. "They can't explain the twinge. I guess a lot of weird stuff happens in pregnancy, but the spotting is normal. We had an ultrasound, and the baby appears healthy—although the doctor has ordered bed rest for Soph the second we get home."

Sophie leaned in. "It's another boy."

He knew it. Colton smiled as his shoulders dropped from up around his ears. "I figured."

"At least we can use Nathan's clothes again." Sophie pressed her hands together. "Now I need to get back to work on the sketches for the sports complex we're building across town."

"No," Jake and Colton said in unison.

Sophie's eyebrow rose. "Huh?"

"Home to bed. The doctor said bed rest." Jake shoved a hand through his thick black hair.

Sophie nodded, still way too pale. "I know, but I can sketch from bed."

Jake nodded. "I guess that makes sense, so long as you sleep a lot, too. We'll need to figure out what to do with your car."

"I had somebody from the ranch go get it," Colton said.

"Thanks," Jake said, his gaze intense.

"No problem."

Jake stepped closer to him. "No, I mean *thanks*. Really."

Colton nodded, his throat closing.

A nurse in pink scrubs bustled out from behind the receptionist with a purple box in her hands. "Mrs. Lodge? These are the new prenatal vitamins we're recommending and giving to all our pregnant patients. Run them by Doc Mooncaller when you see him, but they have a better balance of the calcium and iron, and we really like them."

Sophie took the box with a big smile. "Thanks."

Colton escorted them outside and to Jake's truck. "I need to go close down the office but will head home afterward. Call me if you need anything."

They drove off, and Colton stood for a moment, letting the cool breeze calm him. Across the street sat a bar, and he really wanted a drink. But he probably wouldn't stop at one, and the last thing he needed was Quinn arresting him for a DUI once he'd driven back to town. So, with a shrug, he headed for the empty ice cream store next to the bar. It was probably too cold to eat ice cream.

He greatly enjoyed his double scoop of mint chocolate chip and was almost calm by the time he'd finished the cone. Buying a small vanilla cone in case Tyler still played at the office, he turned toward the door.

Right in time to see Melanie exit the gynecologist's office—with a big purple box of prenatal vitamins in her hands.

He faltered and dropped the vanilla ice cream on the floor.

Chapter Six

Melanie tucked the box of prenatal vitamins in her purse and ducked her head against the wind as she headed toward the jewelry store to return Loni's brooch. She texted Brian to meet her at the store, hoping they could grab a latte.

She returned the brooch and turned around to run straight into Brian's mother. Ug. "Hello, Mrs. Milton."

Mrs. Milton slid her designer sunglasses off her Botoxed face. "Melanie." She glanced around the store. "Looking for rings, are we?"

Melanie forced her smile to remain in place. "No. Are you?"

"Of course not. A lady doesn't buy herself rings, dear." Condescension dripped from the woman's tone as she glanced down at Melanie's jeans and boots, which were an obvious contrast to Mrs. Milton's designer knit suit. "I've been meaning to have a talk with you, anyway."

Well, that was just great. "About?" Melanie asked,

eyeing the door.

Mrs. Milton leaned in. "About your obvious attempts to secure child support for the next eighteen years."

Melanie took a deep breath. "Excuse me?"

"Brian told me about your medical condition, and I have to say, nice try." Mrs. Milton clucked her tongue. "You wouldn't be the first to try to enter my family in such a way, but your manipulations aren't going to work."

Apparently the gloves were off. Melanie leaned down toward the shorter woman. "I believe that's how you became a Milton, right? Knocked up with Brian's older brother?"

Red suffused the woman's pampered cheeks. "Well, I never."

"Oh, I believe you must have." Melanie edged toward the door.

Of course, Brian chose that moment to walk inside. His three-piece suit hung nicely on a fit frame, and his blond hair appeared ruffled. He took one look at the women and sighed. "Afternoon, ladies. What's going on?"

Melanie chuckled. "Well, your mom is ordering me to stay away from you, and my response could be accurately characterized as telling her to bite me."

Brian's grin emerged quick before he sobered, rubbing the smile off his clean-cut, handsome face.

"Brian, I absolutely forbid you from seeing this gold digger. She just wants to raise her station," his mother intoned, obviously not caring who heard.

Melanie snorted. "Station? Listen lady, you live in Billings, Montana, and not upstate New York. High society... you're not."

"I will not sit here and be insulted like this. Brian, I'll see you back at the bank." With a loud sniff and her nose in the air, Mrs. Milton swept from the jewelry store.

Brian grimaced. "Did you have to get in a fight with my mom?"

Melanie shrugged, starting to feel guilty. "She started it."

Brian eyed the lone woman behind a counter showcasing sparkling sapphires. "Hi, Maisey. I don't suppose there's any way you could keep this little family argument quiet?"

Maisey pushed cat-eye glasses up her nose and patted her long gray hair. "Not a chance, Brian. Not even a remote of a chance." Her grin sported fancy dentures.

"That's what I figured. Have a nice day, ma'am." Slipping an arm across Melanie's shoulders, he escorted her back into the weak sunshine. "My mom does have her good points, you know."

The poor guy didn't even sound like he was convinced of that. "I know, and I'm sorry I let her bait me. But why did you tell her about my doctor's visit?"

"I didn't. I researched endometriosis on a computer at the bank, and she saw it. So I kind of had to explain." He sighed. "What did the doctor say?"

"Nothing, yet. He took eggs, and I'll find out tomorrow if they're viable to be frozen. So someday I may have my own genetic kid. Maybe." She tried to keep her voice light. The medical bills were killing her, but what choice did she have?

"Getting pregnant right now might be the solution," he said, stopping the walk.

At that second, her relationship with Brian clarified with a sharpness in her mind. She smiled. "Please don't tell me you're willing to knock me up just to escape your mother."

He chuckled, his brown eyes twinkling. "The idea does

have merit. But, no. I was thinking we should give it a shot for us. For a good future together." As proposals went, it was as lukewarm as possible.

"I like you." Which was the absolute truth. But when she envisioned her future, he wasn't in it. Or rather, he was in it as a friend—a good one. "But we're not in love."

"Are you sure?" Brian sobered. "Give me a chance, Melanie."

She didn't love him—and tying them together with a child would hurt them both. "I'm sorry."

He sighed, the sound full of regret. "So this is it?"

"Yeah." Dating him had been fun and comfortable, but after one kiss with Colton, she wanted that feeling again. Maybe not with Colt, but with somebody. Somebody who could knock her socks off. "I'm sorry."

Brian's head lifted while his lips pursed. "Don't be. I'm fine."

Even so, she'd hurt his ego and not his heart. Speaking of which—"I wish you'd follow your heart." *Lame line, Mel.*

"I have a heart?" Brian asked.

"Of course." She turned and tugged on his lapels for the last time. "You left it on a beach in Malibu during college. Go back there…start a surf shop…and enjoy your life. It's too short to spend behind a banking counter when you don't want to be there."

A faraway look came into his eyes. "But my family—"

"Will understand you have your own dreams. Besides, you have three brothers. Statistically, one of them will like numbers." If not, they should all go find their damn bliss, as far as she was concerned.

"I'll think about it." He brushed a good-bye kiss on her

forehead. "So, friends?"

"Absolutely." A slightly insulting expression of relief crossed his face. Breaking up would probably help him with his family, especially his tyrant of a mother.

Melanie turned away to head for her truck, her mind spinning. Her boyfriend was now her friend, her sexy best friend was now occupying her dreams, and her body was betraying her.

Fate had a cruel sense of humor.

• • •

Late afternoon, after driving back home, Melanie finished the last of her hot chocolate while walking down the main street of Mineral Lake. She'd had to dig for change in her empty pocketbook, but she'd found enough for the small treat. Folks strolled along storefronts, emerging from restaurants and coffee shops, all bundling up against the Montana winter. Warmth was a myth this early in March.

One woman pushed a baby stroller, and Melanie's heart thumped hard. She saw babies everywhere now. Freezing her eggs so she could someday have a baby was a logical decision, even though it emptied her pocketbook.

"Melanie?" a low voice called from behind her.

She turned to find Colton and Leila standing hand in hand.

"Hi, you two." Her lips faltered as she tried to swallow. Colt had such a way with kids.

Colton grinned. "We're glad we spotted you. Join us for dinner."

"Thanks, but I know it's your special night. I'll let you

two get back to your date." She grinned at Leila, who'd worn a pretty yellow jacket and jeans for the big night. Her long black hair was up in pigtails, and she'd put on pink lip gloss. "Your date is lovely, by the way."

Leila grinned. "You're pretty, too. Come to dinner with us."

"Oh, no. I wouldn't want to impose." Melanie needed to get the heck away from her too sexy friend. Just let her libido die down a bit, and things would get back to normal.

Colton reached for her elbow. "Have you eaten since lunch?"

"Well, no. But I'll grab a burger or something on the way home."

"No." He propelled her into Sally's Restaurant. "You need to eat healthier, Mel."

She swallowed. "What in the world is wrong with you?" Colton Freeze had never given one fig about her eating habits.

He glanced at Leila and then back at Mel. "We can talk about it later. For now, we're here, and we're all eating a healthy dinner." He turned toward a row of long booths by the window. "Pick a table, Leila, my girl. Any table you want."

Leila danced ahead and scooted into the booth. "I get to sit by Mel," she called out.

Colton waited patiently.

Melanie thought about arguing, but suddenly she was hungry. And curious. Very curious as to what had gotten into Colt. Maybe the new health kick had something to do with opening up the gyms. "Fine. But you need to stop acting so weird."

"I'm just getting started," he muttered as they slid into the booth across from each other.

The waitress bopped up to take their drink orders.

"Pop?" Leila asked hopefully.

"Lemonade or water," Colton said. "For all of us."

Melanie frowned. She could use come caffeine, but understanding Colton's need to steer Leila into a healthy zone, she nodded. "The lemonades here are fresh."

"Good." Colton leaned forward. "How's your garden at home?"

She smiled, relaxing. "Excellent. I had a great crop last summer and canned a bunch of fresh fruit and vegetables." She loved gardening—from the planting to the harvesting. As a hobby, it was a productive one.

Thus began an interesting dinner of Colton pointing out the healthier alternatives to just about…everything. He even managed to cover the necessity of sleep and exercise.

By the time they walked down the street toward the old-fashioned movie theater, Mel was more bemused than irritated. "Have fun at the movie."

Colton slipped an arm around her shoulder. "You have to finish the date with us, right Leila?"

Leila grinned up. "Yes. We get popcorn at the movie."

Colton faltered. "Well, the salt might be too much."

Melanie stopped cold. Last time he was home, she'd caught him with what could only be termed an orange lunch. Cheeseburger, Cheetos, and macaroni 'n' cheese. "What in the living daylights is wrong with you?"

He shrugged, color filling his high cheekbones. "Salt makes people retain too much water."

Melanie glanced down at her jeans. "Do I look like I'm

retaining water?" She shrugged out from under his arm and looked up into his face. "And be very careful with your answer here, Colton Freeze. I have no problem kicking your butt in front of your niece."

Leila giggled. "That sounds fun."

Colton backed away in the snow, his hands up. "No. You look great." His gaze swept her head to toe and warmed enough to heat the air around them. He swallowed, and his voice lowered. "Really great."

A ball of need unfurled in Melanie's abdomen. How did he do that just with his voice? "Okay. So, let's go to the movie, have popcorn, and even candy."

"Yay!" Leila jumped up and down.

Colton opened his mouth and quickly shut it. "Good enough."

They started back down the street until Mrs. Hudson stopped them. Single, elderly, and sweet, the widow lived at the end of Main Street and was always present. "Why hello, young folks. You out for a date?"

"Yes," Leila answered for all of them.

Mrs. Hudson nodded her gray head and smoothed down her fluorescent green coat. "I heard you broke up with the Milton boy, Melanie. He's a nice boy, but probably not the right one for you."

"They haven't broken up," Colton said slowly.

Mel cut him a look, not surprised the gossip had already reached town. "Actually, we broke up this afternoon, but we're still friends. It's all good." Then she stepped back at the fire shooting through Colt's blue eyes.

His jaw hardened, making him look dangerous. Deadly even. "Why didn't you say something?" The soft tone of voice was all the more frightening for the anger behind it.

Melanie blinked. "I don't know. It actually wasn't that big of a deal. We've been just friends for a while, really."

Loni and Tom Freeze suddenly emerged from the coffee shop. While Loni was dark and petite, her husband was broad with sparkling blue eyes that Colton had obviously inherited. They'd both bundled up in colorful scarfs.

"Off to the movie, folks?" Tom asked, his gaze focused on his youngest son.

"Not a big deal?" Colton asked, his gaze remaining on Melanie. "I'll kill him. I swear to God."

Melanie stepped back from the fury. "Why? I'm telling you, we're fine. What is wrong with you?"

"Son?" Loni asked, sliding her hand along his visibly vibrating arm.

"This isn't okay, not at all." Colton gentled his voice. "I'll talk to Milton tomorrow and work everything out. I promise."

Aliens had abducted her best friend, because there was no way Colton would act like this. "Have you had a stroke recently?" Melanie spit the words out between clenched teeth, her temper awakening. The conversation in the middle of the street with onlookers was just too much.

"Funny, and no." He lifted his chin. "There is no way you're breaking up, and Milton is stepping up if I have to beat him senseless."

That was it. "You have lost your freakin' mind. Get the heck out of my business and right now." She put her hands on her hips.

"No." He continued to ignore everyone around them.

Enough. She jerked away from him. "I'm out of here.

Call me when you regain your sanity."

"You're not going anywhere by yourself. You're upset, and I'll take you home." His voice went guttural with temper as he whirled her back around.

"Why in the hell would I need a ride home?" she yelled, her temper springing loose.

"Because you're pregnant," he yelled right back.

The world halted. Several couples turned around from various positions on Main Street to stare. Mrs. Hudson slapped a hand over her mouth. Tom went still. Loni whirled toward Melanie, and Leila clapped her hands together with glee.

Melanie's mouth opened and closed, but no sound came out.

Chapter Seven

"You are one stupid dumbass," Melanie said on the way to Billings the next day.

"That's the general consensus," Colt agreed from the driver's seat of his Ford pickup. "Again, I'm so sorry I announced to the town that you were knocked up by Milton."

She hunched her shoulders. "It's not just that. Now the whole town knows I'm having female problems. Jimmy Balbie at the bank asked if I needed to sit down while I was waiting to make a payment earlier this morning. When I turned around, he actually stepped back like I was going to hit him."

Colton's lips twitched. "I'm sorry. Again."

"Whatever. You know the only reason I'm letting you drive me to my appointment today is because I couldn't say no to your mother," Melanie muttered.

"I'm fully aware of that." Colton eyed the rearview mirror

and signaled to exit the interstate.

Loni had quickly stepped in the previous night to sort out all of the confusion. Then she'd made sure everyone in town was clear that Melanie was not pregnant.

Colton cleared his throat. "Did you know there's a town bet on what day we get together?"

Melanie glanced up. "*We* as in you and me—we?"

"Yes."

"Are you kidding?"

"No, and I almost didn't bring it up, but I figured you'd want to know. I'm not sure who's taking bets, but I will find out." Colton parked the truck at the clinic. "So what's going on today? Exactly?"

Melanie took a deep breath. Might as well tell him the truth. "They harvested eggs from me yesterday, and today I find out if they are strong enough to be frozen for future use."

"Um, okay." Colton unfolded his large frame from the truck and crossed to open her door. "This explains the money problems you're having."

She nodded. "No health insurance, and these tests cost a fortune. You're right—I'm dead broke."

One eyebrow rose. "You could've asked for help."

"This is personal." She couldn't believe he was even here with her. "Although it is nice of you to bring me to my appointment."

He helped her from the truck. "You're not getting naked or anything today?"

"Nope." Just his saying the word *naked* made her want to strip.

"I'd like to come in with you to talk to the doctor. I have

questions." Colton shut her door and pressed his hand to her lower back in a touch that was both reassuring and possessive.

The touch zinged right between her legs. God. What was wrong with her? She had enough problems without getting turned on by Colton Freeze. Well, she'd tell him anything the doctor said, so why not? "Okay."

"Great. So why do you have prenatal vitamins, anyway?"

Melanie shrugged. "Just in case, I guess. They're giving them to anybody even considering getting pregnant."

"I see." They checked in, and the petite twenty-something receptionist smiled at Colton like they were old friends.

"Back again?" she asked.

He returned the grin. "Can't stay away."

"With your wife this time?" The woman appraised Melanie.

"She's the only woman in the world for me," Colton returned easily. He ran his hand down Melanie's arm as they turned for the seating area in a way that sped up Melanie's heart while asserting a connection.

As if they were a couple—a real couple.

He'd filled Melanie in on Sophie's adventure the previous day on the way into Billings. How frightened the woman must've been.

"I'm glad Sophie is all right," Melanie whispered, although the waiting room was currently empty.

"Me too. Though she may kill Jake if he doesn't stop hovering."

"Poor Sophie," Melanie said, keeping her voice level. What she wouldn't give to have a hovering husband who cared about her health, about her future. She eyed Colton. He'd make a great husband someday.

He caught her glance and reached down to twine their

fingers together. "Stop worrying. It'll be all right."

His palm enclosed hers in warmth and security, sending electricity up her arm to zing through her chest. She glanced down at his darker skin against her much smaller hand. While she was by no means petite, compared to Colt, she was small. Feminine. Her nipples peaked. Thank goodness she'd worn a bra today.

She had to get herself under control. One little kiss, and she was looking at Colton under a different light. One that included nude, moving parts. Although a part of her was beginning to think…what the hell. Why not make a move and take a chance?

The nurse broke her from her internal musings by calling her name and escorting them back into a doctor's office with two leather chairs facing a massive teak desk. A plethora of diplomas decorated the walls along with a couple of pictures of the doctor holding huge rainbow trout.

Dr. Jordan leaned forward, his gray eyes serious and matching his beard. "Please have a seat." He smiled. "I didn't realize you'd be here, Colton."

Colt settled Melanie and then sat down. "I'm here for moral support."

"Good." The doctor paused to read papers in an open manila file.

Melanie's pulse quickened, and a rock dropped into her stomach. She shifted uneasily.

Colton took her hand, and the world settled.

The doctor pushed his glasses up on his forehead as he finished reading. "None of the eggs were viable for cryopreservation. I'm sorry, Melanie."

Cold washed through her. She blinked and then nodded.

Pain lanced along her empty abdomen.

Colton leaned forward while keeping her hand. "Why not?"

The doctor steepled his fingers under his chin. "Tons of reasons. It might be premature ovarian failure, but I won't know why or how without genetic research."

"Even then, you probably won't know, right?" Colt asked.

Melanie's head was in a cloud as she turned his way.

"I researched fertility," he said.

"Maybe." The doctor's glasses dropped back into place. "We may have harvested too early, however. We can try again, but I'm still concerned about the endometriosis. Even if we successfully harvest eggs, you have a small window where I believe you'll be able to carry a child."

"Right now," Melanie said quietly. The emptiness in her grew to pain.

"More than likely, and you probably have about a five percent chance right now." The doctor winced. "Although new treatments are coming forth every day for infertility and endometriosis. I wouldn't lose hope."

"Thank you." She had to get out of there before breaking down. Tears choked her throat. She retrieved her hand and stood. "I need to think about options and will be in touch." As if in a dream, a bad one, she hitched through the office and out the door. She was tough, and she could handle this.

A sharp wind slapped her in the face.

She made it about halfway down the walkway before stopping.

Colton stopped beside her and lifted her chin with one knuckle. "It's okay, Mel. We'll figure this out."

It was the gentle tone that broke her. She burst into

tears and barely had a moment to appreciate Colton's *oh shit* expression before he gathered her close, tucking her into warmth and safety.

"I know I shouldn't have hung my hat on cryopreservation, but…" She started crying harder, her face against his hard chest.

He held her easily, gently rubbing her back, his voice reassuring. A strong, masculine calm in the middle of a wild storm. "Let it out."

So she did. Holding on, allowing him to shield her, she cried for the future she'd never have.

• • •

Colton half-pivoted to put Mel between the brick building and his body when the wind picked up in force. He kept his movements smooth and gentle, tamping down on pure frustration.

He'd stand between her and any danger, but he couldn't protect her from this. Helplessness didn't set well with him. At all.

His mind calculated the way to fix things. To get her to stop crying. He had money, and he'd take her to every specialist in the world.

Winding down with a small shudder, she lifted her head.

Tears clung to dark lashes over her pretty brown eyes. Tracks showed on her smooth skin, and suddenly she felt small and delicate in his arms. Vulnerable. Emotion ripped through his heart with the force of an anvil.

He moved without thinking, stepping into her and covering her mouth with his. The kiss was supposed to be calming, to be gentle.

But as she moaned and pressed against him, his mind shut down. He stilled for one tiny second and then gave in. He fisted her hair, tilting back her head, and went deep. Sweeping inside her mouth, taking, claiming.

Need roared through him, and he grabbed the back of her leg, lifting against his hip and pushing her against the brick. Pressing his cock against the heated apex of her legs.

She sighed deep in her throat and rubbed along his length, tilting her hips for better friction. He had to get inside her. *Now.*

His hand was on her breast before he remembered where they were. Who they were.

He levered back, his breath panting, his chest heaving.

Shock and desire comingled in her dark eyes. His gaze dropped to her swollen, pink lips, and he groaned. He'd give everything he owned to have those wrapped around his cock. Just once.

She gasped and let her foot drop.

A couple of ladies passed by behind him, twittering.

Red bloomed across Mel's smooth cheekbones. He stepped back, his brain swirling, his dick trying to punch through his zipper.

She swallowed. "M-my hair."

Oh God. His hand was still clamped in her hair. Slowly, he disengaged, trying not to pull. She winced as he untangled himself.

He should be a gentleman and apologize. The words stuck in his throat. While he may be feeling a lot of things, sorry wasn't one of them. Not even close. But he retreated and gave her some room.

A myriad of expressions crossed her face, and he read each one clearly. He'd always been able to read her, even when she hadn't wanted him to. Desire, confusion, embarrassment, need…every emotion he was feeling flickered in her eyes.

He took a deep breath. "I promise I'll fix this, Mel. Trust me."

Chapter Eight

Trust me. Melanie shook her head as she left the coffee shop in town the next day. The man was certifiable—there was no way he could fix her situation. He'd driven her home the previous night, and they'd each stayed lost in their own thoughts. The silence had been heavy with way too much thinking, but neither had broken it.

He had to be regretting attending her appointment and then kissing her. Of course, it was the emotion of the moment. No way did Colt want more from her than friendship.

But he sure as hell hadn't kissed her like a friend.

Loni Freeze stepped out of Millard's Mercantile across the street and waved. "Hi, Melanie." Hustling across the quiet road with several packages under her arms, the woman smiled. "What's up?"

Melanie grabbed a package before it hit the icy ground. "Nothing. Just wandering and thinking."

Loni scrunched her nose. With her smooth skin and dark

hair sprinkled with gray, she looked too young to have four grown children. "About anything in particular?"

Melanie shrugged. "About everything."

"Ah, I've been there. Sometimes you just have to relax and let your subconscious take over." Loni eyed Paul's Pizza Joint, which proudly took up several window fronts next to the mercantile. "Let's go grab pizza and figure this out before it starts snowing again."

On cue, Melanie's stomach rumbled. "Okay." She followed Loni into the restaurant, and they agreed on a loaded veggie pizza.

Loni yanked out her phone and typed in letters. "Let me text Sophie to see if she wants a pizza. The poor woman is going crazy on bed rest."

Melanie smiled. "I'm sure. In fact, I don't think I've ever seen her rest." The blonde was a whirlwind.

"Yeah—she's struggling. But that baby will be worth it. I have to say, being the grandmama is a lot easier than being the mom." Loni took a sip of her iced tea. A glint of amusement lightened her dark eyes.

Melanie probably wouldn't be either. She swallowed and tried to smile. "I bet."

Loni's eyes softened, and she reached out to pat Mel's hand. "Everything will work out, sweetheart. I promise."

Melanie flashed back to the third grade when Loni had stepped in. "Do you remember that teacher, Mrs. Simpson? My third grade math teacher?"

Loni sniffed. "I would hardly call that woman a teacher. She sure didn't last long here."

No, she hadn't. Melanie had been staying with the Freezes while her grandfather was on a cattle run, and she'd brought home a math paper with some pretty harsh grading and a request for Melanie's *guardian* to visit the teacher.

Loni had dressed to kill in a business suit and accompanied a quaking Melanie to the school. Then she'd politely waited until Mrs. Simpson, a twice-divorced redhead who spent more time on the single male teacher-parent conferences than anyone else in the history of the school, finished complaining how Melanie couldn't concentrate on numbers and just daydreamed. That maybe she should be put back to the remedial math program of the previous grade.

Melanie, dressed in her best Sunday-school dress, had hung her head, ashamed Mrs. Freeze would realize how dumb she was.

Then Mrs. Freeze had let loose.

Without raising her voice, without using swear words, Mrs. Freeze had calmly explained if there was a problem, it was with Mrs. Simpson's lazy, irresponsible approach to teaching, which was more in line with speed dating. If Mrs. Simpson wanted to catch husband number three, trolling in the elementary school was the wrong tack.

It had taken Melanie several days to figure out what *trolling* meant.

Then Loni had expressed, in great detail, how intelligent and hardworking Melanie was, and that she would someday be highly successful. Loni had wound down with strongly encouraging Mrs. Simpson to try harder as a teacher.

There may have been a veiled threat or two in there, but Melanie didn't read between the lines for several years.

They'd marched out of the school with both of their heads held high. It was in that moment Melanie figured out two things: one, Colton had the best mom in the whole world. And two, she'd never be alone. She was safe.

Then they'd spent several afternoons after school learning multiplication in a way that involved horses, cookies, and hair barrettes. Melanie had gone on to excel in math and even took a college math class while in high school.

Even years later, Loni was Melanie's hero. Melanie smiled. "You took care of Mrs. Simpson, didn't you?" The woman certainly had the clout to get a teacher removed.

Loni shrugged, her eyes sparkling. "Don't know what you mean."

"Thanks for standing up for me."

"Your grandfather would've done the same thing if he'd been in town, although, I do have my own style." Loni laughed. "Plus, you were a great kid, and that teacher was rotten."

It was nice to have people in her corner. Melanie had missed the fun times at the Freeze house when she and Colton had gone their own ways as teenagers. Somewhat, anyway. Colton and Hawk had always been her backup, even when they'd all been dating other people. "Thanks."

Loni leaned back as the pizza was brought to the table. "No biggie. So, how are you holding up?"

"Good." And she realized it was true. Sharing her problems and bawling all over Colt had actually made her feel better. "I wish the whole town didn't know, but…oh well."

"Ah, sweetie. The town always knows." Loni slipped slices onto their plates. "It's good that you and Colton are there for each other. I like that."

Melanie took a bite and chewed thoughtfully. Warm,

gooey cheese landed in her stomach, and she sighed in pleasure. "By the way, have you heard anything about a bet involving Colton and me?"

Loni coughed and quickly took a sip of iced tea. "Bet? What bet?" Her eyes opened wide.

"Oh, come on." Melanie snorted. "You're terrible at bluffing. Please tell me you haven't actually bet."

"Of course not." Loni grinned. "I wouldn't jinx things that way."

Now that was just sweet. Loni had never hidden her affection for Melanie, nor her wish that she and Colton would get together. She'd also never meddled or tried to push them together.

Melanie sighed. "How much is the pot?"

Loni leaned forward and dropped her voice to a whisper. "I heard the kitty is at about five grand."

Melanie gasped. "Are you joking?"

"Nope."

"Who's the bet taker?" Melanie asked.

Loni shrugged. "I'm sure I don't know."

Yeah, right. The town always knew.

. . .

Colton drove into town and slid into an icy parking slot before unfolding from the truck.

"Colton." Mrs. Hudson emerged from the coffee shop, her gray wool coat swallowing her, and a bright pink knit scarf wrapped around her neck several times. "Do you have a minute?"

He hustled toward the elderly lady. "Yes, ma'am. What

can I do for you?" Last night he'd already apologized for the mix-up with Melanie.

Mrs. Hudson slipped her bony arm through his. "We can chat while you escort me toward my car." Her worn boots matched her scarf, and he made a mental note to make sure she got some new boots before snow arrived again. From the chill in the air, it wouldn't be long.

"I'd love to escort you." He angled his body to protect her better from the wind. The woman lived at the end of Main Street and had driven three blocks instead of walking. Rain or snow, the woman always walked, probably so she didn't miss anything on the way. "I noticed you drove instead of walked today. Are you feeling all right?"

"Yes, I felt like a drive today. Plus, it's going to sleet, and I didn't want to get caught." She twittered and patted his arm. "You're such a fine young man. My niece, Beatrix, is visiting at the end of the week, and I was hoping you'd take her out and show her the town."

The woman had always been a matchmaker. He smiled. "That's kind of you, and I appreciate your thinking of me, but I have plans."

Mrs. Hudson slowed down. "Well, she'll only be here two weeks, and I have to admit, she's quite easy."

He coughed out air and glanced down at tight, gray curls. "Excuse me?"

She looked up and squinted faded blue eyes. "Beatrix. She gets around, a lot." Mrs. Hudson shrugged. "I thought you two might have some fun for a couple of weeks before she leaves. Just two weeks."

Colton stopped. What in the world? Realization smacked him in the face stronger than the wild wind. "Mrs. Hudson.

You wouldn't have entered a bet regarding Melanie Jacoby and me, would you have?"

Mrs. Hudson brushed invisible lint off her coat. "Of course not."

Colton bit back a laugh. "Tell me the truth, or I'll go propose to Mel right now."

Mrs. Hudson gasped, her head shooting up so she could meet his gaze. "You wouldn't."

"Oh, I would."

"Fine." Mrs. Hudson sighed. "I have St. Paddy's day as my date, and I sure could use the money, Colton Freeze. If you'd just declare your love that day, I'd really appreciate it."

He couldn't believe she'd tried to bribe him with a slutty niece. Mrs. Hudson was a pimp. He laughed. "I will certainly keep your date in mind. Who's taking the bets and keeping the money, anyway?"

"Can't tell you," she said sadly. "When you make the bet, you have to swear not to tell, or you forfeit your money."

When he found the bet taker, he was going to kick some ass. "What happens if your chosen day passes?"

"You get to make a new bet." She tugged him back into moving toward a blue compact with new tires. "Then you give new money and have to make the promise again."

"Those are lovely tires, Mrs. Hudson." Colton escorted her around to the driver's side.

"Thank you. I won the raffle for new tires at the sheriff's station," she said proudly, opening the door and slipping inside the driver's seat.

Quinn had made sure she won after having bought the tires for her in the first place. "You're a lucky one," Colton said.

She nodded. "Have a nice day, Colton, and remember who covered for you in the fifth grade when you picked flowers from Mrs. Leiton's garden. She's still wondering who took her prized tulips, and as you know, she has a terrible temper." Shutting her door, Mrs. Hudson drove down the street at least ten miles under the speed limit.

Good lord. Mrs. Hudson was a blackmailing pimp.

Chapter Nine

Melanie gave one last chance at arguing with Loni about the check for lunch. "It was my turn to pay."

"I don't think so." Loni stood and then stopped. "Oh. Colton's here."

Melanie turned. Colton had obviously been working the ranch, dressed in faded jeans, cowboy boots, a dark T-shirt, and a black Stetson. As he strode toward her, he looked more sexy villain than smooth good guy.

Hence the black hat.

Heat spiraled into her abdomen.

He kept his dark blue gaze on her, but he kissed his mama on the cheek.

Loni patted his arm. "I have an appointment, but I think Melanie was considering dessert."

No she hadn't been.

"Good." Colton took Loni's vacated seat and removed his hat. "We need to talk anyway."

Loni all but beamed as she exited the restaurant.

Melanie focused on him. "I'm handling my own life."

Colt slowly lifted one eyebrow in a curiously dangerous way. "There's nothing wrong with leaning on friends."

Frustration heated her lungs. "When did you start seeing me as some helpless female?"

He studied her for a moment. "I've never seen you as helpless, and I've *always* seen you as a female. You were a cute little girl, a pretty teenager, and now you're a sexy woman."

Heat climbed into her face, sparking her breasts on the way. "You're giving me a headache."

He grinned. "That's the opposite effect I want."

"What do you want?" The words rushed out of her, and she both wanted to know and didn't want to know the answer.

"Right now I want to help you have a baby."

The waitress gasped as she approached the table. In her twenties, she'd dyed her hair a fun purple to match her eye shadow.

Melanie took a deep breath. The statement would be all over town within minutes. "Julie, I'll take the chocolate sundae with extra chocolate, please." The pizza place didn't sell liquor, or she'd order tequila.

"Vanilla scoop in a bowl," Colton said without flicking his gaze from Melanie's face.

Julie almost tripped over her sensible shoes as she hurried from sight. Probably to start texting friends.

Melanie shook her head. "I-I don't, I mean, you—"

"Not with me." Colton grinned.

A surprising disappointment swirled through her. "Oh.

Of course not."

Colton sat back and blinked. "You don't want to, ah, have a baby with me, do you?"

Okay. The complete alarm he was trying to hide wasn't exactly complimentary. "God, no," she said. Having his kid and just being his good buddy would only cause heartache for her, especially when Colt finally fell for somebody. Somebody *not* her.

He frowned. "Okay." The word sounded a bit disgruntled.

She cleared her throat. "Um, I'm fairly certain the waitress misinterpreted your statement and is now texting everyone in town you offered to knock me up."

Surprise lifted his eyebrows. "Are you sure?"

"Oh, yeah. Definitely."

"Hmm. You wouldn't classify the statement as a declaration of love, would you?"

Good God, her friend had lost his freakin' mind. "No."

His expression cleared. "Good."

She blinked several times, searching for reality. "Why?"

"The bet. When I declare my love for you, the bet ends." He stretched his neck.

Flutters cascaded through her stomach. Love? No. No way. "Says who?"

"Mrs. Hudson. She needs me to do so on St. Paddy's day and tried to bribe me with an easy niece." Colton grinned.

The flutters turned into wild batwings. His smile was too much…just too much. Melanie swallowed. "That's terrible."

"Maybe." Colton leaned forward and grasped her hands.

Fire shot through her with an electric arc. "W-what are you doing?"

"I called the doctor for more information earlier, and

your window is short, Mel. If you want to have a baby, now is the time."

She was the last Jacoby alive, and she'd wanted to have a baby. To keep her family alive. But at what cost? She'd felt all right freezing eggs, but to get pregnant right now? There was no other choice if she wanted to have a child. "I may go to the sperm clinic in Seattle." Sure, a lot of women did it. But she wasn't sure it was fair to plan on being a single mom.

"Perfect. I have a list of specialists you can see in Seattle, as well." His thumb stroked her palm, and she bit back a groan of need. The touch was light, sensual, and way more erotic than she would've dreamed.

"Well, I guess I might head to Seattle." Right? She hated that her body was forcing her into this decision when she wasn't ready. But deep down, irritation welled at how accepting Colt was about her becoming pregnant. Maybe it was because they wouldn't know the sperm donor? Or maybe he really did only see her as a friend and didn't wonder a little bit about them, like she did.

Colt released her and leaned back when the waitress delivered their desserts. "I'll see if we can lease Henry's plane for the ride."

Private plane? Henry's car dealerships succeeded all over the Pacific Northwest, and he owned a private jet that flew him around when he wanted. At about ninety and crotchety, the guy didn't travel much any longer. "Um, *we*?" Melanie slipped her spoon into the chocolaty mess.

"Sure." Colt tried his ice cream, his gaze thoughtful. "You shouldn't go alone, and I can combine the trip with some business. I'm still worried about that firm I invested in heavily, so I'd like to see if I can fix the situation."

Melanie started. "How heavily?"

He sighed. "Enough to have me concerned, but I'll take care of it. Plus, on the plane, we can review the plans for the gym. I'm picking them up from the architect later today."

A plane ride, in a private jet, with sexy Colton…to go get inseminated with somebody else's sperm? Gee. Now that sounded like a vacation come true.

Melanie forced a smile. "Can't wait."

• • •

Thunder bellowed across the wide Montana sky outside, and Melanie hustled around the ranch house to grab flashlights and candles. She loved a good winter storm. Since the temperature had warmed up, they probably wouldn't get full snow. But sometimes the rain became spectacular.

The house had stood proudly in place for generations and would easily weather the storm. Two stories, it held three bedrooms on the top floor, while the living areas were on the main floor. Her grandfather had raised her in the family home after her parents had died in a plane crash, and sometimes she still felt his presence.

Today while she'd mucked out stalls, she'd sang his favorite Garth Brooks tunes. God, she loved ranching. Love the smells, the sights, even the uncertainty. She'd never want to do anything else.

She flicked off the kitchen lights and wandered into the large living room. A stone fireplace took up one wall, while a wide bank of windows framed majestic mountains out the back. It was barely dusk, but soon the clouds would cover any remaining sun.

She'd donned comfortable yoga pants and a heavy shirt for the evening show. Placing her warm coffee on a table, she tucked herself into an overstuffed chair with an ottoman to watch the storm.

As if Mother Nature had waited just for Melanie, lightning sparked a fluorescent purple over the snow-white mountains.

Beautiful. Absolutely stunning.

The skies opened with a crack, and icy rain slashed down.

Lightning jagged across the sky again, illuminating the creek outside the window. She gasped and rushed to the window. Waiting. Another flash, illuminating a massive heifer tangled and kicking ice.

Panic coughed up Melanie's throat, and she slid her cup onto a table. The creek wasn't frozen all the way through, and if the cow didn't stop kicking, it'd plunge to an icy death.

How the hell did it get so close to the creek, anyway? Grumbling, Melanie threw on a jacket, hat, and gloves before grabbing a flashlight and wire cutters from the entryway table. She opened the door and ran smack into Colton.

He grabbed her arms to keep her from landing on her butt. "Where are you going?"

"To save a heifer." She eyed the raging storm as her garbage can slammed up against the side of the nearest barn. "Want to help?"

"Of course." He shut the door. "Where?"

"This way." She led the way down the porch and jogged around the house toward the almost frozen stream. Rain pounded down, soaking her hat. She shivered and plunged along the snowdrift. "What are you doing here, anyway?" she yelled over the violent wind.

"Came to talk about the trip tomorrow," he yelled back, shielding her from the storm.

Melanie swung the flashlight toward the flailing cow. Crap. It was one of the few pregnant cows, so not a heifer. She couldn't lose both the cow and the calf. The cow bellowed in anger as its powerful hoofs smashed ice in every direction.

"Whoa there," Melanie murmured, sliding through snow. "Calm down, baby." Barbed wire cut into the cow's neck as it fought, its eyes a wide, wild brown. "She must've fallen through the fence up the hill."

Colton wiped rain off his forehead, peering closer. "She brought part of the barbed wire with her." He squinted, focusing up the hill. "Ice slide."

Melanie turned to shine the flashlight up the hill just as the cow broke away from the ice. With a bellow, the animal leaped toward them. Melanie caught her breath on a stifled scream.

Strong arms wrapped around her, throwing them both to the side. They impacted ice and mud, sliding several feet. Colton rolled them over, holding her tight, taking the brunt of the damage, the side of his face smacking against the ground.

Snow and dirt whipped around them.

Melanie coughed out air and lifted her head, her body flush on top of Colton's.

"You okay?" he asked, brushing pine needles from her hair.

She blinked, her heart racing, her breath caught. Everything had happened so quickly. The body beneath her felt harder than the frozen ground. His scent of musk and male overcame the smell of pine and storm, and warmth spread through her chilled skin. "Yes."

"Good." Blood flowed from a cut above Colt's right eyebrow. He rolled them over and stood up. "Stay here." Taking the wire cutters from her stiff hand, he stood and stalked over to the cow, now fighting with a pine tree that had caught an edge of the barbed wire.

Melanie scrambled to her feet, her boots sliding on the mud.

Without wasting a moment, Colt dodged in and tackled the cow, one knee to its neck, the other on its flanks, careful to avoid its belly. Sure movements had the barbed wire snipped in several places and removed. "Stand back, Mel," he called over the storm.

She nodded and retreated against the side of the house.

Colton jumped back, and the cow struggled to its feet and snorted. For the briefest of moments, they looked at each other. Then the cow turned and ran toward the nearest pasture. "We'll probably have to hunt her down after the storm," Colton yelled, turning around.

Melanie nodded again, her body rioting. She could only gape as she focused the flashlight beam on her best friend.

He stood in the rain, blood and mud mixing with water across his chiseled face. Wet cotton clung to his hard frame, and passion all but cascaded off him.

He turned her way and…grinned.

Her heart clutched. In that very second, two things became frighteningly clear. One: she didn't know her best friend as well as she thought, because his smile masked the nature of a truly dangerous man. And two: she was completely and forever in love with him.

Chapter Ten

Colton forced his hands to unclench and his voice to remain calm. "Are you all right, Mel?"

She nodded, her eyes too wide in her too pale face. "Yes."

Frustration swept through him, and he fought to keep calm. The sight of Mel's frightened face would keep him up for nights. She shouldn't be managing a ranch all by herself—accidents always happened.

He strode through the storm, grasped her arm, and began leading her back to the house. "Are you all right?" he asked, once he stepped onto the covered front porch.

"Me?" she laughed, the sound slightly off-kilter. "You're bleeding."

He wiped blood off his forehead. "Just a scratch." Clearing his throat, he tried to stomp mud off his boots while tugging a clean bandana from his inside coat pocket to wipe his hands clean. "I, ah, need a shower."

She stepped toward him, and he lifted an eyebrow. After

what seemed like a small mental debate, she grabbed his destroyed shirt and tugged. Stretching up on her toes, her mouth slid against his.

Fire lashed through him so quickly he swayed. A million thoughts exploded at once, and he shut them down. Completely.

Groaning, he hauled her close and took over. The fear, the storm, the fury all comingled into raw need inside him. There were no more thoughts, no more uncertainties.

There was only this woman and this moment.

So he took both as deep as he could. He angled his mouth, and she drew a sharp breath, holding it.

Her lips softened beneath his as he explored her, learning her taste. Wild huckleberries and brandy? The most delicious combination in existence. She moaned deep in her throat, the sound sparking down his torso to his balls.

Her grip on him was strong and sure. He bent her, his hands full of woman. Brushing a hand across her firm ass, he shuddered. "Do you know how long I've wanted you?" Punctuating his words, he cupped a handful. Firm and tight, her flesh was better than he'd dreamed.

He shouldn't have said that. But the connection between his mouth and brain had disappeared.

She sighed against him, pressing closer. "Hurry."

"Hell, no." He reached behind them to shove open the door, backing her inside. Heat blasted them. His hold tightened, and he lifted her to sit on the rugged entryway table, legs spread, shirt now muddy and wet.

The storm raged outside, rain clashing down past the covered porch. He kicked shut the door. Even so, the wildness inside him overtook any sense of caution. Of reality.

Letting go of any doubts, he fisted her hair and twisted, putting her right where he wanted her. She returned his kiss, gyrating against him, the calm Melanie turning into a wildcat.

Her nails bit into his coat. She unclenched her hold and released him in a primitive display of trust.

He wouldn't let her fall. God, this was Melanie. He gentled his touch, leaning back. Slowly, he ran his knuckles across her smooth cheekbone. "You're beautiful," he breathed. The woman mattered, and he'd take care of her.

She blinked, freezing for a second. Then her eyes darkened, and she yanked on the hem of his coat and shirt, pulling both up and over his head. He ducked his head and allowed her to tear it off. The cold wind slapped his skin right before her warm palms slid across his pecs.

She breathed out and pinched his nipple.

He stilled. Heat spiraled through him, and he allowed himself one small breath. Control. He needed control. Glancing down at her upturned face through heavy lids, he felt the first snapping of it spinning away.

Her eyes were melted chocolate and glazed with need. He'd bruised her lips, and they pouted pink and gorgeous. But he needed to slow down and show her how much she meant to him.

Much more than he'd be willing to admit to either one of them.

Keeping her gaze, he slid a hand over her undulating abdomen and down into her yoga pants, not stopping until his fingers touched a very thin cotton barrier. Swallowing, he moved the material aside and found her.

Hot and wet, her soft skin almost dropped him to his

knees. Tapping his fingers in place, he wrapped his other arm around her waist and lifted her. She slid both arms around his neck and pressed closer, her thighs hugging his hips, her core tilting against his hand. A soft moan of need escaped her, and his cock zipped to full attention.

Holding tight, he headed straight for the sofa to sit her on the back. A quick twist, and he yanked her shirt over her head.

Oh God. She was perfect.

Small, white, and sweet, her breasts tempted him. Teased him. He dropped and licked one pink nipple, circling the bud until it was hard as glass. The intimacy of the moment caught his breath.

She dug her hands into his wet hair, holding him close. His Mel wasn't shy.

He tried to restrain his strength, but she pulled on his hair, and gentleness became a dream. She keened when he scraped his teeth across her nipple.

So he turned to the other one and gave it the same attention before standing upright and grabbing the waist of her pants. Her hands drifted down his body to his belt. "Lift," he whispered.

Releasing him, she balanced on the back of the sofa with both hands and lifted. A cloud, a tinge of uncertainty crossed her girl-next-door face as he removed her pants and thong.

That wouldn't do.

He dropped them to the ground and kissed her, hard and complete. She moaned against him, and he pressed against her sex, sliding one finger inside a warmth too hot to be real.

Her breath caught even during the kiss, and she pushed against him.

He released her and waited until her eyes focused before speaking. God, she was amazing. "Hold yourself up, Mel. If you fall, I stop."

Confusion clouded her features until he dropped to his knees and his mouth found her.

Her entire body went rigid, and for a moment, he thought she'd fall onto the sofa cushions on the other side. But her thigh muscles tightened, and she remained in place.

He grinned against her, his finger working her G-spot, his tongue lashing her clit. She tasted like the forest, wild and free. Those spectacular thighs trembled, and her internal walls gripped his finger.

The minx was fighting it.

Amusement and determination filtered through him at the same time. Only Mel would try to control when and how she orgasmed. She was about to learn that any control in the bedroom belonged to him.

He sucked her clit into his mouth, and at the same time, he slipped another finger inside her to twist.

She cried out, her back arching, as she came. Her abdomen trembled while she rode out the waves. He lashed her clit, prolonging her orgasm as long as he could.

Finally, with a murmured sigh, she came down.

And fell over the back of the couch.

• • •

Melanie sprang to her knees and shoved wild curls away from her face as she gaped at Colton on the other side of the sofa. That had been the most amazing orgasm of her life. By the pleased look on his face, he knew it. She had no words.

Mud coated his pants, and Colton's cheek had swollen with a purple bruise. Even so, she wanted him inside her. Now.

As if in total agreement, he unbuckled his belt and drew it through the loops. The hills and valleys of his rigid abs compared to those of the mountains around them. Powerful and dangerous. Then his jeans and boxers hit the floor. He held a condom in his right hand. Good. Definitely a good idea.

She swallowed, not sure where to look. Now that she'd orgasmed, reality was threatening to return. She dared a peek.

Holy fucking crap. The rumors whispered by lucky cheerleaders in high school were true. Beyond over the top, true.

Colt was built. Gifted. Freakin' huge.

She swallowed. "Um—"

"Stop thinking." He reached for her waist and lifted her over the sofa.

"Man, you're strong," she muttered, that damn fluttering setting up in her abdomen again. He'd lifted her like she was one of those delicate, fan-waving women in the city.

"Strong enough." He spun her around to face the couch. Seconds later, he pressed her against the leather.

Panic and desire swooshed through her. "Colt—"

"Shh." He nipped her ear, his body enclosing her, his heated breath warming her skin. "Open for me, Mel." A smart slap echoed before her ass radiated an erotic pain.

She opened her mouth to protest—probably—and he cupped her sex, his index finger tapping her clit. *Oh God, Oh God, Oh God.* She tried to push up, to do anything, and was stopped by his free hand flattening across her upper back.

"I want you like this," he whispered into her ear, sending tendrils of lust through her skin. "Just like this."

A crackling filled the air as he must've slipped on the condom. Grasping her hips, he plunged inside her with one strong stroke.

She cried out and levered up on her toes, taking all of him. He was too big—too wide—

He reached around and tugged on her clit, and she dropped down. The fiery need lashing through her forced her to push against him, to gyrate, to do anything to ease the pressure.

"Relax, Mel." He slid his hands over her bottom, caressing where he'd smacked her. "I've dreamed of my palm print right here." Then those dangerous fingers slid around and up to her breasts to play.

He tugged and caressed, sending sparks of electricity to where they remained joined.

"Colt," she ground out. Emotion swamped her. Colton Freeze was inside her. Completely. Her heart jittered, and she tried to control herself. "Move or I'll kill you."

"Hmmm." He licked along the shell of her ear. "Like this?" Slipping his hands down, he grasped her hips and slowly slid out of her to smoothly slide back in.

"M-maybe a bit faster," she panted, her vision going gray. "So I don't have to murder you later."

"Ahhh." He nipped. "Okay." Dark amusement lowered his voice. Digging his fingers in, taking control, he slid out and then back in with force. Increasing his speed as well as his strength, he began to pound.

Hard, angled, and in perfect timing, he thrust into her.

They moved in tune with each other, instinct and history whispering something neither would accept right now.

She arched and tried to take him deeper. So deep he'd never find his way out.

He chuckled and planted his hand against her upper back. She tried to push harder, to get him to quicken his thrusts, stilling only when a hard slap across her buttocks shocked her.

Wetness spilled from her, coating her thighs.

"I don't like that," she hissed against the cushions.

"Liar," he whispered, his grip strong and sure.

With his hand holding her in place, and his body thrusting, she could do nothing but take what he was giving. Helpless, she couldn't move, she couldn't even see him behind her. Damn if that didn't turn her on more.

The moment held a powerful truth. He controlled more than her body.

With a low growl, he pounded harder, his dick swelling inside her.

She sighed, arching, trying to reach the pinnacle. "Colton."

He slowed, and her eyes flipped open.

Then he paused.

She shook her head. No stopping! Digging her nails into leather, she shoved back against him.

He chuckled at her ear and slowly withdrew to turn her around. "I want to see your face," he murmured.

The tenderness and fire lighting his amazing eyes stole her breath. The shift from wildness to Colt's natural sweet disposition threw her, and she swallowed.

He threaded both hands through her hair and leaned in. The kiss started soft and instantly spiraled to lava. She rubbed against him, the ache inside her almost unbearable. He lifted her to slide them both to the other side of the sofa. The second her butt hit cushions, she manacled his hips with her legs, securing her ankles.

One strong thrust, and he imbedded himself inside her.

She opened her mouth on a strong exhale. "I've always wondered," she whispered.

A gentle smile curved his lips. "Me too."

One more soft kiss to her mouth, and he reached down to grab her hip. Slowly, he started to move.

Electricity ripped through her. "More."

His eyes darkened with an emotion she couldn't read. His pace increased along with the force of his thrusts.

She curled her fingers around his rib cage, digging in. Her thighs clenched. But she couldn't look away. A part of her wanted to look away, to sever the intimacy binding them tight, but he held her gaze captive.

All or nothing.

That was Colt.

A spiraling whipped through her, slamming hard in her cervix, and she cried out, her back arching. Waves of intense electricity rippled through her, and she held on, riding them out. His name was the only sound on her lips.

Finally, with almost a sob, she went limp.

Colton ground against her as he came. Enfolding her, he kissed her cheek. "Melanie."

Chapter Eleven

Colton checked his blackened eye in the bathroom mirror after wiping away fog. Dark and purple. Yep. He'd had worse, but it was still a shiner.

Melanie combed out her wet curls next to him, her silence speaking volumes.

After having sex, they'd washed up in her tiled shower, and it was all he could do not to take her again. But he'd been rough, and although Mel thought she was tough, she had a delicacy that had always concerned him.

The moment held intimacy, and a part of him wanted to dive right into it. Sex with Melanie was different. Better than anything he'd felt before…more real.

But this was *Mel*. And they'd had *sex*. He made sure the towel was fastened tightly around his waist before turning toward her. "Are you all right?"

She started and glanced up at him. Pink wandered across her cheekbones. "Fine. You?"

The crisp tone nudged his temper. "Yes. Did I bruise you?"

She whirled toward him, fire lancing through her eyes. "You mean when you *spanked* me?"

God, she was pretty. Stunning even. The challenge all but shooting from her had the dual benefit of ticking him off and amusing him. The woman was trying to deflect the situation, and a part of him didn't blame her. So he stepped into her space. "If I had really spanked you, darlin', you'd know it."

Her outraged intake of air was his only warning before she smacked his thigh with the hairbrush.

"Ow." He rubbed his skin. "You're a brat."

"Maybe." She went back to brushing her hair, her teeth sinking into her bottom lip. "I don't know what to say."

Shit. Neither did he. His usual urge to run after sex was nowhere to be found. Instead, he wanted to grab her again and spend the day playing in her bed. All day. "What do you want to say?"

She frowned. "I'm not sure. Part of me is freaking out, part is happy, and part is wondering if I just betrayed Hawk."

Colton swallowed. "Hawk?" His mind reeled. "I mean, you and Hawk haven't—"

Melanie snorted. "Of course not. Jeez. But the three of us make a friendship."

"I know." Colton's shoulders relaxed. The idea of Mel and Hawk had hit him in the gut. Hard. "He told me to go for it before he left."

Mel arched an eyebrow. "Go for it?"

Heat rose through Colton's face. "Not in a juvenile way, but in a good way. That he likes our friendship but has always thought you and I might become more."

"Are we? Becoming more?" she asked, chocolate eyes darkening.

"I don't know." Well, if she could dig deep and be honest, so could he. "Do you want to become more?" God, what was he asking? What did he want? He needed to step back and think a little. Come up with a good plan.

She grinned. "Look at your mind spin."

He settled. "What do you want, Melanie?"

She blinked. "I, ah, well, things are a little odd right now. With going to the sperm bank and all."

No shit. "I know." He rubbed the bruise at his eye. "For now, why don't we just take it easy? I mean, let's keep this between us until we figure things out."

She nodded, sending curls flying. "I don't want to lose our friendship. We aren't in a position to take this beyond anything more than friends with benefits," Mel said. "And yes, I know how wrong that sounds. But we have to swear when this thing ends, we will stay friends for life. Definitely keep it between us. The last thing we need is gossip."

"Exactly." He expelled a deep breath.

"Um, do you still want to come to Seattle with me?" she asked.

Frankly, he had mixed feelings about the sperm bank. "I wish there was more time to figure this all out."

"Me too." She slid the brush onto the counter. "At first, I was just being smart by wanting to freeze the eggs. But now, if I don't give in vitro a try, then I might never have a child."

"What about adoption?"

She shrugged. "That's certainly an option, and a good one, but I'd still like to get pregnant. Just once. Maybe see my mother in a baby, you know?"

He nodded. "I'm definitely going to Seattle with you."

"Because of the business problems."

He shook his head. "Because you need support. Dealing with the business problems is a bonus."

She grinned. "Stop flirting with me."

"I'm not flirting." Although he appreciated her attempt to lighten the mood.

"God. You don't even know when you're flirting." She grabbed his towel and pulled.

He reached for the material, only to have her laugh and run out of the bathroom, leaving him buck-assed naked. If she thought that would stop him, she didn't know him at all.

Grinning, he leaped after her with his battle cry echoing.

Her laughter turned to near giggles as she ran through the house in her towel, almost tripping but never quite slowing down enough for him to pounce. Figured that intimacy with Melanie would be fun as well as sexy as hell. This was new.

The front door shot open, and Colton turned to block Melanie from any threat.

Quinn stood framed in the doorway, water dripping from his hat.

Colton choked back a laugh. "Hi, sheriff. What's up?"

"I heard a scream." Shocked would be an accurate description of Quinn's expression. "Where the fuck are your clothes?" Slowly, he turned his head as Melanie padded out from the kitchen, still wearing her towel. "Oh."

Melanie clutched the towel to her breasts. "Morning, Quinn."

Quinn flushed ten shades of red. "Mornin'."

Colton bit his lip to keep from laughing out loud. "What's up?"

Quinn tapped his hat against his leg, sending droplets flying. "Um, some of Melanie's cattle wandered down to our eastern pasture, and I thought maybe she had a fence down."

"She does." Colt scratched his head and caught the towel Mel threw at him. He wrapped the material around his waist, keeping his gaze on his brother. "Go get dressed, Mel." Suddenly, he really didn't like anybody, even his brother, seeing Melanie half-dressed.

Relief crossed Quinn's face. "Good idea. Then we can, ah, figure out which fences need repairing." Quinn waited until Melanie headed into the bedroom to pin Colton with a hard stare. "What in the hell are you doing?"

Colton lost his grin. What the hell was he doing?

Chapter Twelve

Melanie straightened her seat belt in the private plane as they prepared to land. There were four rows of plush leather seats, each with a table in front of it. She and Colton were the only passengers, and he sat across from her and to the left. After a long morning of mending fences on both ranches, they'd swung by his cabin for clothes, and they'd headed for the plane.

Where Colton had plunked furiously on his laptop.

They hadn't talked, and she wasn't quite sure what to say, anyway. He was all but obsessed with his meeting, and she studied him as he pounded away on the laptop even now.

She'd never seen the business side of him—not really.

He'd made several phone calls during the short flight, and the financial numbers he'd rattled off had been impressive. For once, the charming cowboy had been replaced with a genius shark now wearing a suit.

A black suit that emphasized his size and strength in a

way that dampened her thighs. She glanced down to make sure her bra was working. Yep. Any evidence of her arousal was safely hidden. Thank goodness.

He clicked the laptop closed, and she jumped.

One dark eyebrow rose. His mask of charm had disappeared and left a man staring at her with an intensity that sped up her breath. In the darkened plane, the blue of his eyes took on a midnight hue. "We should talk about last night," he said.

"No." The word emerged—an instant defense against anything he could say. She settled her hands on her flowered skirt. "Thank you, though."

His unwavering gaze remained on her. "Yes. We're involved, and now you're heading to a sperm bank. I used a condom last night—"

"Ofcourseyouusedacondom." She breathed the words out as quick as she could. "God, Colton. I'm not asking you to get me pregnant."

He wet his lips. "I know. But things have changed, and I, ah…"

Things were certainly complicated. Melanie cursed her body for putting her in this position. Her heart ached. "Are you saying if I have somebody else's baby you don't want to see me? I mean, we're not really seeing each other. One night…that wasn't even a night. I mean, it was one orgasm. Okay, two for me and one for you. But—"

"Jesus, Mel. Take a breath." He leaned back. "I care for you, I—"

"Stop." The last fucking thing she needed was him to let her off easy. Hurt flowed through her, and she shoved the pain away. "Last night was just sex, Colt. One time, and it's over. There's no need to feel obligated, nor is there a reason to ruin our friendship. Let's forget it."

He finally blinked. "I don't want to forget it."

Her head jerked up, and her lungs heated. Unwelcome and warm, hope coiled through her chest. "Huh?"

"I just want some time. To ease into this and figure out what it is. I mean, it's *us*."

She forced her shoulders to relax. There was no logic here. "I know."

"So let's explore the new us." He straightened his understated tie. "I've dated a lot of women—"

"I know that, too," she said dryly.

He shot her a look. "But none of them have meant an iota of what you mean to me."

Her heart thumped. Hard. "The problem is I don't have time. Not really." If she ever wanted to have a baby, now was the time. Even so, chances weren't good. At the thought, she finally accepted this path. She'd do everything she could to have a baby.

He shoved his hand through his hair. "I know. But—"

The wheels set down with a minor thump, and they were on the ground. He sighed and unbuckled his belt, waiting until the plane taxied to the private hangar before standing and swiftly opening the door. He held out a hand. "I have a car waiting."

She halted in standing and then took his hand. He wouldn't have a limo, would he? No way could she go to a sperm bank in a limo. No way. "My life is becoming a bad sitcom." She followed him down the steps.

"What?" Colton asked, turning around.

"Nothing." Relief filled her at spotting the black Camaro

waiting by the plane with its top already down. Seattle had been experiencing a very nice March with an ever present sun, unlike Montana. "Nice car."

He grinned. "I thought you'd like it." Accepting their overnight bags from one of the two pilots, he tossed them in the trunk.

Melanie slipped into the passenger seat, taking a moment to appreciate the smooth leather. "I still don't understand why we needed to bring overnight bags. We're heading home today, right?" In addition, she might leave town knocked up. She blinked. No matter what Colton said, her becoming pregnant should put a damper on whatever they were starting together. If they were starting something. Chances were—

"Mel. Stop thinking so hard." Colton unfolded his length into the driver's seat. "My meetings may go late, and we might have to stay the night. I promise I'll make it worth your while." The deep timbre of his voice slid right under her skin to spring nerves to life.

"Stop flirting with me." She buckled her seat belt.

"I'm not."

Goodness help her if he started. She sighed. "Now isn't a good time for us to start something."

"Yet we did." He ignited the engine and smoothly drove the powerful car through the quiet private airport to the main road. "It's not like you're getting inseminated today, anyway. This is a preliminary consultation, right?"

She swallowed. "Normally, but with my circumstances, they said they'd expedite the process if I want. I made the appointment months ago in case the embryo freezing didn't work, and they would have all of my files and history by now."

"Oh." His hands visibly tightened on the steering wheel. "I'll cancel my meeting and go with you."

"No." Panic tasted like acid. "If I'm going to do this by myself, be a single mom, then I should do it all by myself." The idea of Colton sitting outside the door while she had her feet in stirrups, changing her entire life, made her head spin. "Thanks, though."

He cut her a look that shot straight for her panties. What was wrong with her? God. She couldn't arrive at a sperm bank turned on.

Life had gotten too weird too quickly.

Would she go through with it? For the first time in weeks, she wasn't sure.

. . .

Colton ignored the spectacular view of the Seattle skyline outside the conference room window, his mind spinning. He shouldn't have dropped Melanie off at the sperm bank. But she'd insisted, and he really didn't have a right to accompany her.

Melanie. Pregnant. Not with his kid.

Which one of those statements bothered him the most? He hated to admit it, especially since they'd never even been on a real date, but if there was a kid in there, he wanted it to be his.

What the fuck was going on in his head?

The last thing he'd planned on at this stage of his life was settling down. Sure, it worked for his brothers, but he was just getting started in his career. Frankly, he'd liked playing the field. A lot. His plan was his plan, and the idea of altering it sent chills down his back. Plus, well, it was Melanie. She deserved somebody established in life, somebody ready to take care of her.

He'd be that guy if his plan went along the correct course, but not for a while. Right now, he was just starting out—and he may have already screwed up.

But when he thought of forever, when he thought of something real, the only face he saw in his head was Melanie's.

There wasn't anybody else he wanted to plan life with. To wake up with every morning, and to grow old and cranky with. Only Melanie.

And he'd just dropped her at a sperm bank alone.

"So what do you think?" Mark Manning, the CEO of Greenfield LLC asked, shoving his wire rims up his pointy nose.

Colton frowned at the only other person in the conference room. "About what?"

Mark sat back, his scrawny neck moving. "About our financial shortcomings. Can you invest more money?"

Colton leaned forward and made sure he had Mark's attention before replying. "No."

Mark sighed. "Then I'm not sure what we'll do."

Colton flipped open the report in front of him and grabbed his pen. "You'll reallocate these resources here… and these here." He proceeded to step-by-step show Mark how he'd not only climb out of the red but start making money.

Mark finally sat back. "I think you're right."

Colton smiled while keeping his eyes hard. "I know.

Also, you should be aware if you ask me for more money again, I'm going to shoot you."

Mark laughed and quickly sobered, his light brows slanting down. "Are you serious?"

"Yes." Okay, he wouldn't shoot Mark, but he might beat the crap out of him. "I told you not to invest in the other natural-oil company, and you didn't listen. Now I have to go back to my board of directors and tell them times are going to be tight for the next year." His board was his family, and he hated letting them down. But after the tough year, he'd work his ass off until times would be flush again, hopefully.

A flush time he'd like to spend with Melanie. The woman had never traveled. He'd love to take her somewhere warm for a winter vacation, somewhere they could find a private beach and play nude. Those breasts would probably burn. God, he loved her breasts.

His head jerked up. He had to stop her. If she needed a baby, he'd give her one.

Standing, he quickly shook Mark's hand. "I have to go. Send me weekly reports until we're back on track." Ignoring Mark's look of surprise, he hustled out of the office and all but ran for the car parked on the street.

Would it be too late?

The curse words he hissed as he maneuvered in and out of traffic compiled into a crazy flow of expressions. Where the hell did people learn to drive? Finally, he double parked in front of the skyscraper housing the sperm bank.

Running inside, he scanned the kiosk near the elevators. Fifth floor. She was on the fifth floor.

He skipped the elevator for the stairs, taking them two at a time. He burst into the waiting room, and several people glanced up from filling out forms. Lots of forms.

Long strides propelled him across the room to the receptionist's granite desk. "I need to see Melanie Jacoby. Now."

The receptionist, a buxom middle-aged redhead with deep frown lines, shook her head. "I'm sorry, but she's in a procedure room."

Oh, hell no. His brain had shut down hours ago, so his body took over. He shoved open the door next to the desk and hurried down a long hallway lined with closed doors. His boots echoed on the fake wooden floors.

"Melanie," he bellowed, trying doorknobs.

One door opened to reveal a nude fat guy holding a plastic cup, and Colton yelped, slamming the door. "Sorry, dude. Lock the door." God. That image was burned in his retinas for life.

"Melanie Jacoby," he yelled louder.

A door opened farther down, and Melanie stepped out, pamphlets in her hands and her eyes wide. "What in the world?"

He took a deep breath. "Don't do this. Have my baby instead."

Chapter Thirteen

Melanie took a sip of her wine in the small alcove of the restaurant. The scent of garlic and roasted peppers wafted around. "You are out of your flipping mind," she repeated.

Colton drew air in through his nose, his hand around a glass of some man drink. "I know." He grinned. "But you should've seen the face of the guy I stopped mid-jack."

Laughter bubbled up in Melanie, and she snorted. "I bet you weren't looking at his face."

Colton groaned. "Don't remind me."

After hurrying from the clinic, Colton had driven them to his favorite pizza joint in the outskirts of Seattle. "So you didn't get inseminated."

"No. Even though I'm ovulating right now, I couldn't do it." Frankly, she had been having doubts and was no way prepared to make such a monumental decision. Well, not true. She'd decided to hold off because of Colton. She didn't have to admit the truth to him, but she couldn't lie to herself.

"I don't know what to do."

Colton nodded. "Well, I was thinking. Say you get a baby from a sperm bank, and you have a boy. Who will teach the kid baseball?"

She hunched her shoulders. "Well, probably you, though I'm not bad." Although Colt had been the best pitcher in Montana in high school and part of college before he'd turned to MMA fighting.

"Right. And who will attend those embarrassing *your body is changing* nights at school with him?" Colt took another drink of the clear liquid.

"You." Melanie nodded.

"In other words, if you had a baby, I'd step in anyway."

She sighed. Truth be told, any time she pictured a little boy, she pictured him with Colt's intriguing hair and eyes. "I know." Now she felt selfish for even considering having a baby. She wasn't the only one whose life would change.

"So why not give the kid superior genes and a whole lot of cousins and family?" Colton showed a rare dimple in his right cheek.

Melanie lifted an eyebrow. "Superior genes?"

"I'm glad you agree." Colton finished his drink as the pizza arrived.

She shook her head. "The timing is terrible. I mean, after we—"

Colton slipped pieces on their plates. "I know. The fact that we slept together does muddy the *let's have a baby* waters."

Melanie rubbed her eyes. "Life has gotten out of control." It'd be smoother if she could take that night back, but deep down, she didn't want to. "I can't ask you to become a father right now. I know that's not in your big plan."

"My big plan?" he asked.

She grinned. Self-aware, he was not. "Sure. You plan everything. Go to school, check. Get masters, check. Take over family company, check. Talk Dawn into working there in a year or two, check. Open businesses with childhood friends, check. Play the field and have fun for a decade, check. Find hot, big-breasted blonde and settle down with three point two kids…"

He chewed thoughtfully and then sipped his water. "You know me pretty well, do you?"

"Yes." The pizza warmed her belly, and she finally relaxed for the first time that day.

His gaze heated hotter than the pizza. "You believe in fate, right?"

She shrugged. "Sure. I live in Mineral Lake, Montana. Fate and destiny are in the waters. In fact, I've had a funky spirit guide who looks like a leprechaun ever since I was a kid. He believes in fate, although he believes in making your own."

"Your spirit guide is a leprechaun?" Colt asked.

"No. I don't know what he is. But he looks like a guy who'd guard a pot of gold. To be honest, I think he's a couple cards short of a full deck." But as a guide, she liked Bob.

"So, let's proceed as if we just started dating, which frankly, we have, and see where fate leads us." Colt signaled for another drink. "And we ditch the condoms, and let destiny decide."

She coughed and then quickly took a drink of her wine. Colton—inside her—bare and hard? God. Heat slammed between her legs, and she shifted restlessly. Sex anywhere and anytime with Colton?

She tried to sound normal. "Let destiny decide? That is so unlike you. For years, I've watched you plan every relationship, up to and including the probable breakup."

"I've never been with you before."

Warmth spread right around her heart and settled in. If he didn't stop being so sweet, she was going to fall even deeper in love with him. She cleared her throat. "What if I do get pregnant?"

"Then we proceed from there." Colton accepted his new drink and didn't seem to notice the waitress all but pressing her boobs against his shoulder and flirting.

Melanie waited until the woman had left. "If I get pregnant, you'll convince yourself you're in love with me, and then you'll want to get married to fulfill your plan. I can't take the pressure." Even worse, what if he fell in love with somebody else down the line, and she was left alone? Because from the moment lightning had struck her the other night, it had become abundantly clear that Colton was it for her—and he still saw her as a buddy he wanted to help out.

The sides of his eyes crinkled. "I'd hate to pressure you, so let's make a deal."

Even she knew better than to make a deal with Colton Freeze. "What kind of a deal?"

"If I get you pregnant, I promise not to pressure you to marry me." He leaned back, confidence in his eyes. "In fact, I'll wait until you ask me."

• • •

Colton opened the door to their hotel suite, smiling at Mel's gasp of surprise. A stunning sunset illuminated the Seattle skyline outside the wide span of windows, and she hurried past the sitting room furniture toward them to get a better view.

His manic rush through a Seattle sperm bank had showed him one thing in exact clarity. He cared for Melanie too much not to be there for her and whatever baby she had. As always, he could plan this out. The woman reminded him of a skittish colt he'd trained as a teenager, all big eyes and hot temper.

This whole health problem made her even more reluctant to start up with him, so he'd proceed carefully until he figured out what was best for all of them.

He was good with planning. Melanie deserved someone who could give her the attention she needed. He had to save the family business, which might take years. If she did get pregnant, she'd need someone who could help and support her. That couldn't be him. Being a husband and father took real commitment. He could teach the kid baseball, but the day-to-day, well he wouldn't have the time. It killed him, but he wasn't what she needed. He wasn't good enough for her. The idea twisted his gut.

For now, they'd proceed slowly and have some fun.

He yanked his tie loose and tugged the silk free, unbuttoning the first couple of buttons on his shirt.

Melanie turned around as he was rolling up his sleeves.

Her eyes darkened and widened.

He bit back a smile. The expression crossing her face was one he'd never seen on her. Wary and intrigued. So he continued rolling up his sleeves and stalked toward her.

Slowly.

She swallowed. "I'm not sure about this side of you." Her

words emerged just breathless enough to awaken his cock.

"What side?" He continued toward her.

"You know."

He knew exactly what she meant. But she was going to say the words. He reached her and grasped her chin to tilt her head. "What's throwing you here?"

She blinked. "You've always been a bossy and protective pain, but this *edge*, is almost too much."

God, she was sweet. He liked that she didn't play coy, even when he kept her off center. Nor did she attempt to hide the desire now spiraling through her and darkening her stunning eyes. No other woman had ever come close to this one.

"I have never been bossy." He ran his thumb along her lower lip, letting the softness entice him.

She rolled those eyes. "Baloney. If not bossy, then what?"

"In control." He tightened his hold and slid his lips against hers. Once, twice, a third time. "I like to be in control in the bedroom, and you like giving it up."

She gasped and jerked away. "I do not."

Oh yeah. Cat and mouse. One of his favorite games—and one he'd bet Melanie had never played. He leaned in until his mouth rested against her ear. "Sure you do. I bet you're wet right now."

Her hiss accompanied a two-handed push against his chest. But the intrigue crossing her face didn't lie. "I am not."

"Prove it."

"You are such an ass." She bit her lip against a half smile.

He grabbed her and kissed her hard until she pressed against him, little moans chorusing from her chest. Then he released her. "Watch that language, or I'll do more than one little spank this time."

The clouds slowly slipped from her eyes until they narrowed. "I don't think so."

"I do." He ran his knuckle down the side of her face. "We both know I could have you begging, totally at my mercy, within minutes."

Her gasp should've warned him. "Mercy?"

"Yes." He kept his gaze on her smooth skin.

And thus didn't see her leg shoot out to hook his. She took him down in a quick move he'd taught her about four years previous, turning them until he landed hard on his chest, her strong thighs straddling his back.

Her ass hit his just as she slipped an arm under his neck and pulled.

Then, against all logic, he burst into laughter. Not chuckles, not light amusement, but full-bore belly laughs that came from deeper than his heart.

Her execution of the move was beautiful.

He could barely breathe, his neck pulled back, her arm cutting off his air. The cold wooden floor chilled his skin, while his blood heated with lust.

"Stop laughing," Mel hissed, pulling harder.

He couldn't help it. Tears gathered in his eyes, and even with her chokehold gaining strength, he couldn't stop laughing.

Until she released his neck, grabbed his hair, and smashed his forehead into the floor.

Pain radiated through his entire skull. He stopped laughing.

She. Did. Not.

Using his knee, he flipped over, grabbed her arms, and

rolled until she lay flat on her back beneath him. "That last move is supposed to knock an opponent unconscious," he ground out, his head aching.

She rolled her eyes. "You're fine."

"I didn't teach you those moves to use against me." He fought to tamp down on a temper that suddenly wanted to roar.

"You shouldn't laugh at people. There are consequences." She glanced up at his pounding forehead and blanched.

His temper settled. "You believe in consequences, baby?"

She stilled, her gaze flashing to his. "Uh—"

He reached down, spun them around, and ended up in a position he never thought he'd see, with Melanie Murphy Alana Jacoby over his knee, ass in the air. He brought his hand down hard to gain her attention.

She yelped and tried to scoot away. "Colton!"

He easily kept her in place and laughed, his good humor restored. "You're staying here until you apologize for trying to bash in my skull."

"I should've tried harder." She half-laughed and half-bellowed. "Now let me go."

He smacked her again. "No."

"Damn it." She kicked out her legs. "This isn't right."

He paused. "You're right. This is all wrong." He reached for the waist of her skirt and yanked it off her legs, almost groaning at the sexy black thong that left her pinkening buttocks exposed. He ran a finger along the seam of material. "This is pretty."

"I am so going to kick your ass—" She shrieked as he smacked her again. "Damn it, Colt—"

Smack. "Apologize, Mel." *Smack.* "Though this is fun."

Smack. Smack. Smack.

His dick pulsed in agreement with each playful hit. He settled her more comfortably across his thighs and bit back a harsh groan at the contact. If he didn't get inside her soon, he might explode.

"You're getting turned on by this?" she gurgled, laughing while struggling with all her strength.

"Oh yeah." His palm print was outlined on her gorgeous ass. "I could do this all day. So you might want to apologize." He smacked her again for good measure.

"I should've knocked you out. You're a pervert." She wiggled her butt in a move to slide from his lap, and he groaned out loud this time.

"Pervert?" He palmed her heated ass, grinning at her sharp intake of breath. "You're as aroused as I am."

"Am not," she predictably hissed.

"Lying gets you spanked in earnest." He slid his palm over her butt, between her legs, and fingered her wet slit. Hot and wet, she'd saturated the material.

The sound she made was full of need.

His eyes almost rolled back in his head, and his balls drew tight and said *hello*. He slid up and ran his nail over her clit.

She gasped, her muscles tightening. "Colton."

"Ah, Mel." His voice emerged guttural. "I think I'll make you come just like this. While being spanked."

She shoved her torso up from the floor. "I'm *sorry*. Way, way, way, *sorry*, so *sorry* I smashed in your head, not that you need your brain. *Sorry*, a thousand times *sorry*."

He laughed out loud and then hissed as his cock brushed her underbelly. Well, fair was fair. So he lifted her up.

She turned and tackled him, wrapping her legs around his hips and slamming her ass down on his groin. They both groaned at the contact, and then her mouth was all over his.

Hot, greedy, demanding.

He fell back, taking her with him, his mouth working hers the entire time. Her hands were frantic as she ripped open his shirt, sliding heated palms along his skin.

She fumbled with his zipper, and he kicked off his pants and boxers at her urging.

Levering up, she grabbed him and tried to lower herself. Fire all but shot from her eyes as she failed. "You're too big."

Basketball. Football. Television sitcoms. He fought to keep sane as she gripped him tightly. "No, I'm not." He ripped her shirt over her head for good measure. "Go slower. Take your time."

"Okay." She took a deep breath, and rolled her hips while taking him in.

His heart pounded in his ears, and every muscle he owned tensed with the need to flip them over and pound into her. But he fought the urge, letting her play, allowing her to set the pace.

Finally, decades later, her ass finally hit his groin.

"Oh." Her mouth pursed and her eyes widened. Both palms flattened on his chest as she angled her pelvis.

Heat surrounded him. Pulsing, caressing, taking…her internal walls gripped him with impressive strength. The neurons in his brain may have misfired. Any control he owned was a sliver from snapping completely. "Melanie? You want to start moving now." His voice was raw gravel as he held tight to the reins, uncertain he'd succeed.

"All right." She threw back her head and lifted up.

He manacled her hips and slammed her back down.

Their groans melded together. Then he did it again, setting a pace she easily jumped right into.

He glanced up at her, wanting to stay in this moment forever. Her wild curls cascaded around her classic face, her brown eyes focused elsewhere, and a light blush wandered from her breasts to her cheeks. She was fucking perfect.

Gripping her hips, he set up a fast rhythm. She met him thrust for thrust, her thigh muscles constricting with each movement.

He wanted to slow down, to get lost in her. But electricity sparked down his spine to lash his balls, and he was too close to ending the moment. So he reached down and slid the calloused pad of his thumb along her clit.

She cried out, back arched, nails digging into his chest as the orgasm overtook her. Pumping harder, faster, she yanked him right into heaven with her.

He held her tight, coming like a teenager on prom night.

Finally, she took a deep breath and collapsed against his chest. He slid his palm down her spine to caress her still warm ass. "We're gonna have to do that again," he said with a smile.

Contentment wandered through his blood, warming him. He wanted to spend all night with her in his arms, instead of needing to ease away after sex. Instead of freaking out or worrying about the new feelings, he allowed them to take root.

His phone dinged from across the room. The ding pointed to a programmed alarm. Setting Mel to the side, he yanked on his jeans and scanned his phone.

Shit. A chilling dread slithered down his spine. Melanie

lifted her eyebrows in question, and he shook his head, standing and leaping for the laptop perched on the table. Typing furiously, he double-checked the cash accounts. "Son of a bitch."

"What?" Melanie asked.

"I had an alert set on our accounts with Manning, and it looks like he just took the money and ran." Colton would kick the crap out of him…if he found him.

"Call the police." Melanie reached for her clothes.

Colton sighed and rubbed his eyes. "If we turn him in, the money will be tied up forever as they build a case against him."

"Oh." Her breasts jiggled as she tugged her shirt over her head. "So what's your plan?"

"I go after him." This was a clusterfuck of tremendous proportions. Sure, they could survive without the money for a year by tightening their belts, but at some point, his family needed the money back. Especially before next calving season.

"Okay." Melanie wiggled her butt and shimmied into her skirt.

His dick sprang alive. What the hell? He was facing a complete financial disaster, and his body wanted to play. "You are way too tempting."

The smile she flashed him heated right through his blood to his heart. Man, he needed to get a grip. Turning away, he quickly dialed his assistant. "Anne? Sorry to disturb you. This is what I need." Giving her details, he ran through his itinerary. "Thanks."

Shaking his head, he ended the call and focused back on Mel. "I have to go get our money back."

Melanie nodded. "You will."

"I thought he was my friend. Guess not." How could he have been so stupid? So damn sure of himself he didn't stop to think. Colton eyed the flushed brunette he'd much rather be playing with right now. "You take the plane back home. I have to track Mark down—if he went by car, I'll follow him, or I can get a commercial plane ticket."

"Is this man dangerous?" Melanie asked.

"Not as dangerous as I am."

"Oh." Melanie eyed the door. "I'll get ready to go."

He reached for her and drew her close. "When I get back, we need to talk." Maybe by then he'd figure out what he wanted to say.

Chapter Fourteen

He'd been chasing Manning for three damn days. A biting rain slashed down, competing with the blustering wind. About an hour outside of Fargo, North Dakota, Colton sat in his rented Jeep, gaze on the quiet fleabag motel. Room 117 to be exact.

His contacts at the security firm he often used had confirmed Mark had used a credit card to rent the room. Whoever the firm used as a contact had some serious info, which is why he never balked at their fees.

Colton rubbed his scratchy chin.

A pudgy man following two hookers had entered a room at the farthest end of the motel, but other than that, there hadn't been any life. If Mark was in the room, he was being quiet.

Enough was enough.

Stepping out of the Jeep, Colt's boots splashed in a mud puddle. Striding the distance to the door, he calculated the best approach.

Fuck it.

Planting his boot near the knob, he kicked in the flimsy door. The cheap metal swung open, banging off the side wall.

Mark turned from sitting on the bed, and reached for something in his bag.

Colton was on him that fast, hands fisted in Mark's shirt. "What's in the bag?"

Mark swallowed, his glasses askew on his face. "Nothing."

"Right." Colton tossed the asshole across the room with minimum effort and reached for the barely visible silver gun.

Mark smashed into the dresser and dropped to the floor.

Colton frowned, twisting the gun in the meager light. "This is a Lady Smith & Wesson." He frowned at Mark. "You bought a girl's gun?"

Mark shoved himself up from the grimy carpet and straightened his glasses. He wore a faded T-shirt and dress pants. "You just committed a battery."

Colton grinned and moved to shut and lock the door. Well, shut the door. The lock no longer worked. "You committed theft, fraud, and the worse crime of pissing me off." Turning, he leaned back against the damaged door. "Why are you in North Dakota?"

Mark's Adam's apple bobbed up and down. "I have an investor here and am trying to get all of your money back." He eyed the window and seemed to listen for help.

There was no assistance coming to this dive. Colt clicked his tongue and stepped forward to grab Mark by the neck. "Try again."

Mark's skinny arms moved up to block, and Colton swatted them away. Shit. The guy wasn't even worth it. "I thought we were friends," he said quietly.

Mark sniffed. "We are friends."

"Think so?" Colton threw him into one of two mangy chairs by a Plexi board table. Then he drew Mark's laptop from the gun bag and set the computer before his former friend. "Where's the money?"

Mark shook his head. "The money is gone."

Colton pushed the laptop into place. "Where the fuck is my money?"

Mark wiped his snotty nose on his sleeve. "Gone."

Colton sighed and shrugged out of his coat. "I know you, you little prick. You have an overseas account set up, and now you're going to transfer every cent from that account to this one." He drew a piece of paper covered with a series of numbers from his front pants pocket.

"I can't." Mark sighed, his hands trembling on the table. "You'll never kill anybody over money. Other reasons maybe, but not money."

"You're right." Colton shoved a rough hand through his hair. "I won't kill you."

Mark's shoulders relaxed.

"But I will break every single bone in your body, one by one." He kept his gaze steady. "You think you know me? Keep in mind not only have you stolen from me, you've stolen from my family. That's a hard line you've crossed."

Mark paled. "I'm sorry, but I needed the money. I made some bad bets, and I'm being chased."

"I don't care." Colton leaned down, holding Mark's gaze. "Your problems are yours. Now transfer the money."

"I can't," Mark whispered, his gaze dropping to the silent laptop.

Colton shoved up the sleeves of his T-shirt and sat down at the computer. He hadn't hacked an account since his early teens, but some gifts just stayed with a guy. Even so, it was going to be a long night.

· · ·

Darkness without stars surrounded Colton as he jogged down the airplane's steps in Maverick and tossed his duffel in his truck. Rain smashed down, just as cold as the one in North Dakota.

It had taken several hours for Colton to hack into the accounts, another hour to realize that the actual money was gone, and then two hours to transfer the patents to his family's corporation. The cash was gone, but the patents would pay off. Eventually. For now, he had bad news for his family.

Very bad news.

God, Colton was tired. Threatening people didn't set well with him, and he hadn't slept in nights. The idea of slipping into a warm bed with an even warmer Melanie propelled his foot down on the accelerator.

His phone buzzed, and he frowned. Who would be calling in the middle of the night? A quick glance showed it was Quinn. "Quinn? What's up?"

"Hey. Where are you?"

"Heading into Mineral Lake."

"Good. I'm glad you're home," his brother said.

Colton stilled. "What's up?"

"It's Hawk. His helicopter went down two days ago downrange of Afghanistan."

All thought, all emotion, screeched to a halt inside Colton. The anger over the money, the indecision with Melanie, even his fatigue flew away. "Is he—"

"No. I don't know any details, and Jake is on the phone with his military contacts, but we know Hawk is alive and survived the crash to be brought home. We just don't know where he is right now."

"I'll be right over." Colton pressed harder on the gas pedal.

"Actually, we're meeting at Mom and Dad's in an hour to figure things out. Meet there." Quinn clicked off.

Colton swallowed. Where was Hawk? Why the hell had life gone to shit? He'd had a plan, and he'd been a cocky bastard, now hadn't he? How was he going to fix everything?

There was only one place to go now.

• • •

After being awakened by the doorbell, Melanie opened her front door to find a disheveled Colton standing in the snow. Hollows accentuated his high cheekbones, and fatigued darkened his eyes. Along with pain. "What?" she whispered.

"Hawk's helicopter went down."

Melanie blinked, and half-shook her head. Panic burst through her, heating her lungs. "No—"

"He lived through the crash and was transported to the States." Colton stepped forward and enveloped her in a hug. "We're trying to find out which hospital he may be in right now."

Relief weakened her knees, and she drew in a deep breath of male. "He didn't die?"

"No, and he was healthy enough to bring home to treat, apparently." Colt stepped back. "We're meeting at the main ranch in an hour to figure things out. Get dressed, and I'll drive."

Melanie nodded and scrambled upstairs to throw on clothes. If Hawk were okay, where in the world was he? God, he had to be okay. Too much was changing—way too fast. They couldn't lose Hawk. She finished dressing and ran downstairs to find Colton on the phone.

He clicked off.

She held her breath until he'd turned around.

"Hawk was transported back to the States and checked himself out of the veterans' hospital in Helena. He should be heading home," Colt said.

Melanie frowned even as the world finally settled. "Why didn't he call?"

"That's exactly what we'll ask him when he gets home," Colton said, grim lines cutting grooves into the side of his generous mouth. "I just left him a message to meet at Mom and Dad's. Let's get there before he does."

Melanie nodded and yanked on a coat before following Colton into the storm. She settled against the leather in his truck, turning on the seat warmer. Best invention ever. "How was your trip?" she asked as he started the truck and drove into the blowing wind.

"I got the patents, but we're broke until they pay off." His lip twisted.

She clicked her seat belt into place. "Your family will understand."

"I don't know why they would. I was reckless and stupid." He shook his head as wind hissed against the windows, and marble-sized hail pounded the truck. "My damn plan didn't exactly fall into position."

Melanie studied his hard profile. Why did his plan always have to be perfect? Everyone made mistakes. "They'll support you."

"They shouldn't."

She didn't have any other words to offer. So, turning to watch the wild storm, she slid her hand under his as it rested on the console between them. He tangled his fingers through hers with a tight grip.

Yeah, it felt right.

Ten minutes later, they'd ensconced themselves at the Freeze main ranch house, and Melanie headed to help Loni in the kitchen. Per orders, Mel sliced potatoes in Loni's gourmet kitchen and jerked when thunder yelled outside. The hail turned to blustering snow.

Now she sliced while Loni finished stirring her famous breakfast casserole in a Crock-Pot. Tom Freeze stood next to his wife and kept getting his big hand slapped as he tried to steal a taste of the fragrant concoction. Colton stormed into the kitchen, Quinn on his heels. "He should be here by now," Colt said.

Quinn snagged an apple slice from a platter off to the side. "There was a holdup when he checked himself out of the veterans' hospital outside of Helena. Apparently he did so against doctor's orders."

Now that sounded like Hawk. Melanie slid the potatoes onto a plate. "How badly injured is he?"

"Some internal bleeding, a broken arm, a head injury, and a generally pissed-off attitude," Jake said, loping into the kitchen. "Apparently Hawk refused medical help until they transferred him to Montana, and the second he got there, he discharged himself. I finally got ahold of my buddy in Helena, and he gave me the information."

Melanie sighed, her mind whirling. "Can Hawk do that without getting in trouble with the military?"

"Yep." Jake snaked raw potato. "Hawk was honorably discharged three months ago."

"What?" Colt's head jerked up.

Jake nodded. "He went back as an independent contractor to assist his old unit with something. None of my contacts know what, but well…"

It wasn't a huge secret that Hawk was a sniper. Melanie swallowed. "So he didn't tell us the truth."

"I'll kick his ass." Colton shoved a rough hand through his hair. "After he's healthy."

"That seems fair," Quinn mused.

"So where the hell is he?" Colton growled, punching in numbers on his cell phone again. "He's not picking up."

Quinn rubbed a hand over his eyes. "If I knew what he was driving, or who was driving him, I'd put out a BOLO. But right now, I have no clue."

Juliet wandered into the kitchen, carrying a covered dish. "Sophie is resting in the guest room, and I almost had to tie her down to get her to stay there." Amusement lifted the redhead's lips. "But she says she's feeling better, and the doctor took her off bed rest starting tomorrow."

Melanie's cell phone rang, and she glanced at the screen before excusing herself to the other room.

"Hello, Mr. Carmichael." The elderly man owned the ranch to her east and had been one of her grandfather's best friends.

"Hi, Mel." He coughed for a moment. "I thought I should tell you that several of your Black Angus are wandering around the side of Shilly's Mountain."

Dread slammed through her. "Are you sure?"

"Yep. Used my new binoculars to make out the brand. It's yours." Carmichael coughed again. "Damn allergies, and spring isn't even here yet. So be careful when you head out to fetch the cattle. That mountain ain't safe for them with the coyotes, wolves, and bears."

"True. Thanks, Mr. Carmichael." She ended the call, her mind spinning. At least five fences had to go down in order for those cows to end up in danger. The winter storms had it out for her.

Colton poked his head out of the kitchen. "What's up?"

She turned. "My western pasture has all downed fences. The Black Angus I had settled there are roaming Shilly's Mountain."

Colton lifted his chin and stepped into the room. "There are at least four fences between the pasture and the mountain."

"Five."

"How many head?" he asked.

"About fifty from that pasture." She took a deep breath. "I have to go."

He leaned against the wall and crossed his arms. "What's your plan?"

"I'm contracting with Hawk's crew, so I'll give them a call." Even though he'd been out of town, Hawk's crew remained at work.

Colton nodded. "I assumed you'd call in a crew. But what I'm asking is what the hell you're planning on doing."

She frowned. "They're my cattle. I'm heading out to round them up."

"All by yourself?" His voice dropped to a softness that would provide warning to anybody with a brain.

She sighed. "You're miffed I didn't ask you to help?"

"Miffed?" Fire lanced through his eyes, highlighting all the different hues of blue.

She bit back a laugh. "I've asked you for help plenty of times, but I figured you'd be busy finding Hawk, and I didn't want to pull you away from searching. We need to find him and make sure he's okay."

Colton nodded. "I understand. So how about you stay here and help find Hawk, and I'll head out and gather your cattle. The storm has messed with visibility big-time."

She gaped. "Listen, Colt—"

He held up a hand. "There's a big storm about to settle right over Shilly's Mountain, and I'd rather you were safe here. There's a chance you're now pregnant with my child, and that's how it's going to be."

Holy crap. Amusement bubbled up so quickly she snorted. "*That's how it's going to be.*" Turning on her heel, she chuckled as she headed toward the front door. As much as a jackass as he was being, it shouldn't have surprised her when he grabbed her arm. "Let go of me, or prepare to be a eunuch," she said quietly.

He turned her around, conflicting emotions chasing across his hard face. "What if I asked nicely?"

What if she kicked him squarely in the balls? Man, this new status with Colton, whatever it was, took work. "There's less than a five percent chance I'm pregnant. Even if I were pregnant, I can work my ranch for several months until I'd need to slow down. Considering we just had sex three nights ago, I think I'm safe riding a damn horse." She yanked her arm free.

His stubborn jaw set. "Fine." Turning slightly, he raised his voice. "Anybody want to go on a cattle hunt?"

Chapter Fifteen

Three hours later, Melanie stretched her back atop the stallion, wincing as muscles protested. The snow had slashed down, cold and merciless, for at least an hour. Then the clouds had given the earth a break from the attack, while covering the sun. The world stood still and frozen.

A new set of dark clouds began to roll over the mountain. Visibility sucked. She'd go to her grave before admitting she'd give almost anything to be back in the warm kitchen eating Loni's breakfast delight.

Water dripped from the brim of her hat to her gloves, and she shivered.

Tom gave her the high sign from the other side of the valley entrance, and she nodded. She'd sent Hawk's crew to finish rounding cattle from the nearby roads before heading into the final valley. At least five head had been lost, and she needed that money, damn it.

A bellow echoed before the thunder of hooves ricocheted

off the mountains. At least twenty head ran out, chased by Colton and his brothers. If any of the animals tried to veer out of the path, she and Tom needed to chase them back in line.

But for now, all she could do was stare.

Colton rode full bore, his stallion churning mud, his long coat flapping in the wind. The brim of his dark hat was pulled low, and meager light highlighted slanted features and dark hollows in his face.

His chin remained down, his gaze focused on the cattle. The coat emphasized broad shoulders that narrowed to a tight waist. As he passed, the muscles in his thighs clenched the horse.

On all that was holy, he was magnificent.

There was nothing sexier than a cowboy riding through a storm, controlling a wild stallion.

Sure, he was arousing in his suit with his sharp mind-making deals.

But here, in nature, with him controlling everything wild around him? This was Colton in full force. The more primitive, baser part of his nature.

He was everything she'd ever wanted.

Lightning cracked across the mountain, and her mount jumped. In daydreaming, she'd let up on the reins.

Tightening her legs, she tried to hold on as the horse reared up and then dropped his head.

Almost in slow motion, she sailed over his head and held her breath until hitting the earth. Mud splashed around her a second before pain radiated down her arm.

She shook her head, trying to get her bearings.

As if laughing at her, the sky opened up, and rain began pelting down again.

Colton reached her first, jumping from his stallion and sliding in the mud and snow on his knees. "Mel?" He leaned in close, studying her face.

Heat roared through her cheeks. "Oh God," she groaned.

He slid his hands down her arms. "Where are you hurt?"

"I'm not." Embarrassed as hell, but not hurt. She pushed to stand and winced. "I can't believe I just fell off a horse." Because she'd been daydreaming about Colton. God. She'd never live this down.

"Is she okay?" Tom yelled from the other side.

Colton nodded and waved him on. He clicked his horse into a trot and followed the other two so they could secure the cattle.

Melanie wiped mud off her hands. "I'm sorry."

Colton eyed her, head to toe, leaving tingles in the wake. "Are you sure you're all right?"

"Besides mortification? I'm fine." Her arm hurt, but it was just a bruise.

He tilted his hat up in a dangerously sexy way. "It's stormy, it's dark, and we're all tired. It could've happened to anybody."

Any other man would've given her a *told you so* that she should've stayed back at home when he'd asked. Not Colton. He tried to make her feel better even after she'd made such a rookie mistake. She sniffled.

Alarm lightened his eyes. "Are you crying?"

"No." She sniffed again.

He brushed a kiss across her forehead. "We've all been thrown. It happens. At least you didn't land on your butt and break your tailbone like Jake did. Remember?"

Her grin came naturally. Jake had been showing off for

some girls in high school. "Yes, I remember."

"Good." Colton pressed a proprietary hand to her lower back, steering her to his horse. "Looks like we ride double until we fetch your horse. Keep your hands to yourself, Jacoby."

Now that might be tougher than he thought. After seeing him in full action, she wanted nothing more than to get her hands on him.

His cell phone buzzed, and he yanked it from his back pocket. "What?" Then he stiffened. "Okay. Thanks." Ending the call, he glanced at Melanie. "They found Hawk passed out in the driver's seat of a rented SUV on I-90. He's at Maverick County Hospital right now."

. . .

Colton paced the tiled hallway, his thoughts churning. Every once in a while, he glanced at Melanie as she sat quietly by his mom in the orange waiting chairs of the hospital. Sophie and Juliet took up the other two chairs, while Jake and their dad stood like anchors near the doorway.

Mel was too pale, and she kept favoring her right side.

When she'd been thrown, Colton's life had flown before his eyes. While he'd always thought that was a stupid cliché, it turns out it really happened.

He knew any baby in her hadn't even formed baby parts yet, so there was no way a tumble from a horse could've hurt the forming cells. If there were forming cells. Chances weren't good.

But Mel could've broken her neck.

Sure, she'd been thrown before. They all had. But now

he wanted to smother her in bubble-wrap to keep safe.

This new caring about somebody he was sleeping with wasn't nearly as fun as he'd expected.

The doctor finally came into sight down the long hallway, and Colton met him halfway. "Well?" Colton asked.

"Your friend hasn't regained consciousness," the doctor said, gray eyes tired. "We've requested his medical records from the VA hospital and should know more as soon as they arrive."

Frustration heated Colt's esophagus. "Why hasn't he regained consciousness?"

"I don't know." The doctor rubbed his neck. "Until I see his records, I don't even know what the underlying injury was. I'd like to do an MRI but need to make sure he doesn't have any metal in his body. Thus, the need for his records to get here first."

"I'll make sure you have them within the hour," Jake said, grabbing his cell phone and heading toward the door.

Loni stood and hurried toward the doctor. "How about Hawk's other injuries?"

The doctor nodded. "Your son said Hawk might have internal injuries, and we haven't seen any evidence of that, so that's good news. The arm is broken and has been properly set in a cast."

Loni slid an arm around Colton's waist. "The head injury is the main concern, then?"

"Yes." The doctor sighed. "As soon as I have an idea of what we're dealing with, we can figure out a plan of action. Whether to transfer him or seek an expert here. For now, all we can do is wait."

Colton nodded. "Great. Also, would you mind checking

out my girlfriend's arm? I think she hurt it when she fell from a horse earlier."

All eyes immediately turned his way.

Melanie paled and then stood.

Colton frowned. "What?"

"Did you say *girlfriend*?" Tom asked with a grin.

God, had he? Without answering, he turned and followed Melanie from the waiting area, placing a hand on her lower back in support. She stiffened but kept walking.

"You don't need to come with me," she muttered under her breath.

"Sure, I do." He propelled her along, not liking how she continued to favor her right side.

"You don't trust me to tell you what the doctor says?" she asked.

"Nope." Something in him felt guilty for allowing her to get hurt on his watch, which made no sense whatsoever. If Hawk had taken a tumble, Colt wouldn't feel responsible. But things were different with Mel now, and she was his to protect. If he told her that, she'd rightfully punch him in the face.

So he steered her into the examining room, hoping nothing was broken.

She sat on the crinkly paper and gave him a look. "I have to take my shirt off."

He grinned. "Why do you think I came?"

His smart-ass reply had the desired effect of making her smile. "You're such a perv."

"So you already told me."

At his reminder of the afternoon in Seattle, a pretty blush wandered across her face. He watched, fascinated.

"You have the prettiest skin, Mel."

She laughed and then winced. "Stop flirting with me. I'm in pain."

He instantly sobered and reached to help with her shirt. "How much pain?"

"Not enough to have a doctor take a look," she said.

Colton took a glance at her arm and stilled. "Holy shit."

She looked down. "I told you I was just bruised."

Yes, but the bruise extended from her shoulder and down her entire arm in a range of different purples. He gently pulled her arm away from her body to run his fingers along her ribs. They seemed fine.

The doctor came into the room, and Colton turned around. "She's just bruised. But if she's pregnant, would this injury harm a baby?"

The doctor looked up from a chart to focus on Mel. "How far along?"

She gripped her hands together. "A few days."

The doctor finally cut a smile. "Ah, no. You're safe." He leaned in and examined the bruise, as well as her shoulder and ribs. "The bruise is a doozy, but nothing is broken. I recommend rest, aspirin, and a cold compass." He straightened. "Hawk is still unconscious, but you can take turns sitting with him now."

Colt's gaze met Mel's worried one. Hawk had to wake up.

Mel nodded toward the doorway. "You can go first."

"Thanks." He slipped her shirt back over her head and gingerly slid her arm through the slot. "I'll be back in a minute."

Following the doctor, he forced his face into casual lines

in case Hawk had awakened.

He hadn't.

Hawk overwhelmed the hospital bed, all ripped muscle, his eyes closed and his breathing even. Electrodes attached lines from machines to his body, and the beep, beep, beep of the machines continued in a rhythmic cadence.

Mottled bruises covered every exposed area of his tanned skin. Bruises from fists and what appeared to be a bat.

Fury spiraled through Colton so fast he nearly swayed. The helicopter story was a fucking lie. He knew a good beating when he saw one, and somebody had beaten the absolute shit out of his oldest friend. As soon as Hawk woke up, they'd go seeking justice.

. . .

Melanie studied the soda machine at the hospital's break room, her mind spinning and her arm aching. Colt had called her *his girlfriend* to his family. She had seriously mixed feelings about the statement.

Well, once the thrill of hearing the words had dissipated. Girlfriend. Yeah. That meant they were dating and not just having sex. But girlfriends in Colton's life had expiration dates on their time with him.

From the second she'd realized she was in love with him, caution had kicked in. The guy went through women pretty regularly, and she didn't want any awkwardness with her friends or family when they ended.

Well, if they ended.

What if they didn't end? Her mind could easily spin with

daydreams of happily ever after with Colton. He wasn't an easy guy, but if he gave his heart, it'd be once and it'd be completely.

A rustle sounded by the doorway, and Sheriff Quinn Lodge strode inside. His black hat was pulled low over his handsome face, and he still wore the long coat from riding earlier. "What are you doing in here?"

She shrugged and looked at the closest person she had to an older brother. "Trying to figure out how to make Colton fall in love with me."

Quinn lifted both eyebrows. "I'd bet he's already in love with you. Who wouldn't be?"

Melanie grinned. "You're biased."

"Of course I am." Quinn smiled. "Jake said Colton called you his girlfriend out there. Want me to beat him up for making the assumption?"

What a sweet offer. "Nah. If he needs a beating, I'll take care of it." She sighed. "I just don't want everything to change."

"Change is good, Mel." Quinn tossed his hat on a nearby table. "Usually. Any word on Hawk?"

"No."

Quinn frowned, worry lining his face. He had his mama's dark eyes and hair, but his large build must've been from his daddy. "Hawk is tough. He'll be okay."

"I know."

Quinn leaned and peered at the machine. "Do you have a dollar I can borrow?"

She snorted and dropped quarters in his hand so he could buy a Pepsi. "Thanks for everything, Quinn."

He headed for the door and turned around to shoot her

a quick grin after fetching his wet hat from the table. "I'm just getting started." Then he disappeared from sight.

Melanie grabbed a couple of more quarters and bought a soda. Well, time to do what would piss off the entire family and make the phone call none of them would make. Then, she quickly drew her cell phone from her pocket and pressed speed dial.

"Hello?" a sleepy voice mumbled.

"Dawn? It's Melanie." Mel was pretty sure nobody had thought to call Dawn Freeze at college.

"Mel?" Something rustled, and Dawn's voice gained clarity. "What's wrong?"

Melanie forced herself to remain calm. "Hawk was injured in a helicopter crash, had the navy bring him home, and checked himself out of the Helena hospital. Then, somehow, he was found by the side of the road. He's in Maverick at the hospital and hasn't gained consciousness."

Silence beat over the line for several seconds. "Nobody called me."

"I'm calling you. We're at the hospital right now and don't know anything yet." Melanie kept her voice calm, sure the boys wouldn't have called their younger sister until knowing something. But she would've wanted to know, and so did Dawn.

Dawn gasped. "I'll head home right away."

"That's up to you, but please drive carefully."

"I will. Thanks for calling me, Mel. You're a good friend." Dawn disengaged the call.

"Did you just call my sister?" Colton asked from the doorway.

Melanie gasped and turned around. The man moved

silently enough to be military trained. "Yes."

Colton frowned, harsh lines in his face and anger in his eyes. "Why did you do that? Now she'll drive through the storm to get here."

"So? She's an adult, and she can make her own choices." Plus, she was Mel's friend. "If you were injured and in the hospital, I would fully expect Dawn to give me a call. That's all I did."

Irritation swirled across Colt's face. "We don't know anything about Hawk, and Dawn needs to stay at school. I'll keep her informed."

Melanie coughed as her temper sprang to life. She was tired, she was wet, and her damn arm hurt. She didn't need a lecture from one of Dawn's way overprotective brothers. "You dumb son of a bitch. Dawn has been in love with Hawk since he fished her out of Miller's pond when she was four. She needs to be here."

A flush covered Colton's high cheekbones, and he yanked a cell from his back pocket. "That silly crush was over a long time ago. Thanks for the help, but my family can handle this." Turning on his heel, he exited the room.

Chapter Sixteen

Colton loosened his hands on the stirrups as he led the way through the forest on the edge of their land, finally opening to a wide field. After leaving the hospital, he'd grabbed a few hours of sleep before lunchtime, and then he and his brothers had been repairing fences downed by the storm. "Hey, I was thinking about moving Lodge-Freeze headquarters to Mineral Lake."

Quinn pulled abreast of him on his vibrating stallion. "Works for me."

Jake pulled up on the other side. "The top floor of the Franks building is for lease."

"I know. I actually called Old Man Franks to see if he'd be interested in selling the entire building. Paying rent doesn't sit well with me." Colton eyed the metal barn in the distance.

"How is business, anyway?" Jake asked.

Colton took a deep breath. He'd deliver the bad news

later—when he could tell everybody at once. "We can have a meeting tonight to discuss the upcoming year. Considering Dawn is coming home." Yeah, he was putting off the inevitable as long as possible.

Quinn glanced at his watch. "She should be home in a couple of hours. I guess we should've called her first."

"Yes. She's pissed." Colton drew up on the reins. "Though not as pissed as Mel is. I didn't handle that well."

"You are a moron," Jake agreed.

"You don't want Dawn coming home right now any more than I do." Colton rolled his eyes. "She'll camp out at the hospital, and that's not a good thing."

Quinn growled. "I thought this whole crush thing she had for Hawk was over."

"It is." Jake squinted at the clouds now rolling across the sky. "But they're still old friends."

"What if the crush isn't over?" Colton asked quietly.

His brothers didn't answer him. Hawk was family, and they'd die for him. But the guy definitely had issues after his time in the service, and their baby sister was innocent.

"It's over," Quinn said. "What's up with you and Mel, anyway?"

Colton sighed. He'd been expecting the question. "It's complicated."

"Bullshit." Jake blew out air. "If you're just messing with her, I'm going to mess with you."

Colton nodded. "I figured." If he hurt Mel, he deserved both his brothers trying to kick his ass. Of course, he knew how to fight, too. "I won't hurt her."

Quinn groaned. "I have to ask, and I don't want to sound like a girl, but I have to say the words. How do you feel about

Mel?"

Jake snorted. "You sound like a shrink, not a girl."

"Shut up." Quinn steered his stallion toward a ridge. "Answer the question, Colt."

"I don't know." Colton hunched his shoulders. "She's different than anybody I've been with, and I'd cut off my arm before hurting her. The idea of her with somebody else makes me want to hit something, and when she flew over the head of that horse—" He cut himself off. There weren't words.

Jake smiled and nodded. "He's in love."

"Of course he's in love with Mel—he has been for eons." Quinn shook his head. "He's finally realizing it. Dumbass."

"He's always been slow," Jake agreed.

"Both of you shut up." Colton dug in his heels. "We haven't been dating long enough to be in love. We'll date and then figure it out."

"Ah. The life plan according to numb-nuts." Quinn nodded sagely. "Stick with your life plan, and you're going to lose her."

The thought of really losing Mel, of not having her in his life, compressed Colton's lungs. "I'm done talking about this."

"So am I." Quinn dismounted. "What's everyone's plan for the rest of this fine Saturday?"

"I'm heading home to play with the kids and check on my pregnant wife," Jake said slowly. "How about a barbecue and family board meeting at my house tonight?"

"Sounds good. I have paperwork at the office and then I'm home helping Juliet move paintings around in her gallery." Quinn grinned. "Can't wait for the board meeting."

Colton sighed. "I'm heading to the hospital to yell at Hawk to wake up, and then apparently I'm preparing for a board meeting."

"Will Mel be there?" Jake asked with a sly grin.

"Why? She's not family," Colton retorted. Besides, Mel was so pissed at him right now, she wouldn't even take his calls. Maybe flowers would help.

"You truly are a dumbass," Quinn muttered.

God. People needed to quit saying that. "I'll call when I get a visual on Dawn," Colton said.

He finished with the horses and hurried outside to his truck, taking time to appreciate how the meager sunlight sparkled off fresh snow as he drove through town. The storefronts all showed green decorations ranging from clovers to drunken leprechauns.

Flashing back to their third grade parade, he grinned. Melanie's grandpop had hand-sewn her a mermaid costume that was spectacular. He'd been so proud until discovering that his new-found talent put him in immediate demand for all school plays and festivities.

Through the years, the good-natured rancher had sewn plenty of costumes.

God, he'd been a good man. While Melanie put on a strong face, she had to be missing him.

Colton frowned. He'd been way too hard on her about calling Dawn.

He plotted the way to get her to forgive him as he drove out of town and across the county to the Maverick hospital. Pulling into a parking spot of the hulking wood building, he glanced around for her car.

Disappointment flooded him that she wasn't there.

Sighing, he hustled out of the car and loped into the hospital, winding through hallways until reaching Hawk's room. Once at the door, he stopped short.

Dawn sat in a chair, her small hands wrapped around Hawk's large one. Fear sat in her eyes and along her classic face.

Fuck. His sister was in love. The real kind.

Colton hitched inside, and she turned tear-filled eyes toward him.

He paused again. When had his baby sister turned into such a beautiful woman? Dark blue eyes took prominence in delicate features, while her black hair hung straight to her shoulders in a classic cut.

She stood and hugged him, her grip strong and somehow delicate. The scent of huckleberries surrounded her, and reminded him of home. She didn't even reach his chin, and a wave of protectiveness swept him. "How are you?" he asked.

She levered back and smiled. "Fine. You?"

Actually, his life was a bit fucked up right now. "Great. Any news on Hawk?"

She turned back toward their friend. "His medical records came in, and he's scheduled for an MRI in an hour. Vitals are good, but he hasn't awakened."

Colton slipped an arm around her shoulder and tucked her close. "I would've come to get you."

"I can drive, Colt." She elbowed him in the ribs. "Though you should've called me sooner."

Maybe. "How's school?"

"Good. Finals are in two months, and then I'm done with one more degree. Everyone thinks I'm crazy for applying to Oxford for the doctorate." She shrugged.

He grinned. "You're just wanting to put more letters after your name than I have. In fact, I've been to more of your graduations than my own." He was plenty proud of his baby sister.

She nodded and tugged him toward the chairs. "I wish Hawk would wake up."

"Me too." Colton settled in to support his sister and guard his friend. "I need your help getting Melanie to forgive me."

"She said you were a complete ass," Dawn said.

"I was."

Dawn grinned. "I figured. So, let's plan, and then I'm supposed to help you with the Paddy's Day float."

• • •

Colton cradled little Nathan as he loped over bouncy castles, stuffed frogs, and a smattering of little socks to answer the doorbell. "I'll get it," he called back to Jake, who was busy barbecuing steaks on the back deck.

He'd put everyone to work creating the Dracula-leprechaun-themed float, and it was now ready to go.

Then he grinned at the changes in the house since Nathan had arrived. For so long there were princess and mermaid toys all around for Leila, and now miniature footballs and frogs kept appearing. "I'm glad you're here," he whispered to his nephew, who looked up with huge dark eyes in an already strong face.

Yeah, at about a year old, the kid looked just like Jake.

Colton opened the door and stopped short.

Melanie blinked, her hands full of a huge casserole dish.

"I thought you were at the hospital."

"I was, but Quinn picked me up." He shifted Nathan to his other arm as the boy held out chubby hands for Melanie. "Ah, switch." Taking her dish, he smoothly slipped Nathan into her arms.

She grinned and cooed. "He has even more hair than he did last week." With a sigh of pleasure, she nuzzled Nathan's wild mane of black hair.

Colton drew her inside so he could shut the door. "I'm sorry about earlier."

Melanie glanced up, obviously trying to hold on to her mad. But with a happily gurgling baby in her arms, the battle was a losing one. "I don't want to talk about it right now. Why are you here, anyway?"

"My family likes me," he said easily.

"They have to like you in case they need a kidney someday." She kept her voice soft for Nathan's sake, but spunk still shone in her eyes.

Man, he'd love to meet her challenge head-on, and better yet, in the bedroom. He grinned. "I overreacted, and I hurt your feelings by implying you weren't family. For that, I'm truly sorry."

She blinked twice.

He knew Melanie as well as he knew himself, and she never could resist a sincere apology. He really was sorry.

"Fine." She brushed past him.

Playing stubborn, was she? The evening just became a whole lot more interesting. He inhaled the scent of her famous huckleberry cobbler with a sigh of appreciation and followed her into the chaotic kitchen.

His gaze only dropped twice to her tight ass in curve-hugging jeans. His own jeans suddenly felt too tight.

Dawn hopped off a stool to hug Melanie, the baby sandwiched between them. "Tell me you brought your cobbler," Dawn said, untangling her hair from Nathan's grabbing hands.

"Of course." Melanie glanced around at the abundance of family. "I didn't know this was a family barbecue."

Dawn shrugged and slid her arm through Mel's. "We're having a quick board meeting before dinner, but it's no big deal."

Melanie faltered. "Who's with Hawk?"

Sophie glanced up from chopping a salad on her new granite countertop. "Mrs. Hudson and Mrs. Wilson are with him now, and then the Lady Elks are taking shifts all night. We're back on duty tomorrow."

Colton wasn't sure Hawk would want so many people watching him sleep, but they did want somebody there when he woke up. "Hawk's going to be cranky about this."

Dawn grinned. "I know, right?" Although her smile was genuine, dark worry glimmered in her eyes. "I'd stay at the hospital, but the doctors are adamant that only one person be in with him at a time, and the whole town insists on taking a turn."

"Hawk's tough—he'll be all right," Colton said. God, he hoped that was true. Hawk had to wake up. Soon. "The MRI showed brain swelling, but not enough to do surgery. He'll be fine." If he woke up. The longer he remained unconscious, the greater the chance he'd slip into a coma.

Tom loped in from outside. "Let's do this board meeting so we can eat."

Colton nodded and led the way into his dad's huge study, where he'd left quarterly reports. He served as president of the board, while Jake served as VP, Quinn as secretary, and Dawn as treasurer. Tom was ex-president, so he sat in on the meetings.

Colton cleared his throat. "Are Mom, Sophie, or Juliet joining us?"

"They said to go ahead, that since they're not officers, they don't have to stop having fun," Dawn said with a longing look inside. "They're looking on a website for new baby furniture along with Melanie."

Colton called the meeting to order. His hands sweat, and a knot rolled in his stomach. "I, ah, made a mistake."

His dad sat back, eyebrows raised. "What kind of a mistake?"

God. He couldn't do this. "I got cocky and made a risky investment—we lost money."

"How much?" Jake asked, frowning.

"Too much." Colton cleared his suddenly dry throat. "I hunted down and secured the patents for the green stock I told you all about last year, but they won't pay off for at least a year."

Quinn leaned forward, his hands on the table. "What does that mean?"

Meeting Quinn's gaze was one of the hardest things Colton had ever done. "No dividends for the year—maybe two years."

Dawn gasped, her eyes wide. "None?"

"No." Colton shuffled his feet. "The patents will pay well in a couple of years, I'm sure of it."

Silence echoed around the room for several heartbeats. Colton could almost hear rapid minds kicking facts into place. His ears burned, and a tight knot of regret settled hard in his stomach. Why had he been so sure of his plan?

Finally, Tom sighed. "Then we tighten our belts for a couple of years." He glanced out the window at his sprawling acreage.

Quinn rubbed his chin. "Juliet's just starting to see cash flow at the gallery, but we can make it on my sheriff's salary, even if the ranch takes a hit."

Jake nodded. "I have a couple of good court cases coming up—might even have enough to pay ranch expenses for all of us."

"But you have the baby and medical bills," Dawn murmured. "I can put Oxford off, or take out student loans." She pushed her dark hair out of her face, intelligence shining in her eyes. "Working for a year or two before Oxford wouldn't hurt me any."

Colton swallowed. "I'm so sorry."

Then he steeled himself, prepared for their disappointment.

"We'll be back on track in a couple of years?" Quinn asked, flipping through the report.

"It looks like it," Colton said.

"Will this affect any of the land holdings we currently have?" Jake asked.

"No, but it will affect our ability to acquire more land for the next two years. And, nothing can go wrong with the ranches." Yeah, right. Ranching by its very definition included risk. Colton leaned forward, gauging their reactions. Why wasn't anybody yelling at him yet?

"Good enough." His dad flipped closed the report. "We're going to need your plan."

Colton dropped into a chair. "My plan?"

"Yes." Quinn tossed his report on the masculine coffee

table. "You're our financial guy. We'll get you reports on what we think is coming in for the next year, you figure out expenses, and then come up with a plan."

Jake rubbed his chin. "You are the planner."

Dawn nodded. "We'll just pool our resources. It isn't like we haven't done that before. I'll get a job."

"No," her dad said. "If you want to attend Oxford, that goes in Colton's plan as an expense. Period."

Jake and Quinn nodded.

Colton frowned. "Why aren't you all mad?"

Dawn's eyebrows drew together. "Mad about what?"

"About my crappy business decision that has hindered us." Colton rubbed his chin. "I've screwed up." So much for his grand plan.

"You did go to Seattle, and you fixed it." Quinn tapped his fingers on the wooden table. "Running the entire company is a tough job, and we trust you to do it right. The patents look good, and they'll probably end up making us a lot of money."

Dawn reached over and patted his hand. "Everyone makes mistakes. It's okay, Colton."

Emotion welled through him so quickly he nearly swayed.

"In other words, chill out and give yourself a break," Jake said, leaning back to glance into the kitchen. "Now, could we call the meeting over so I can go prevent my wife from buying out the entire furniture store online?"

Colton swallowed. They trusted him. Shit. They believed in him. "The meeting is adjourned."

As he glanced around at people who'd support him no matter what, he was struck with how lucky he was. He wanted to share that…with Melanie.

Chapter Seventeen

Melanie breathed in the chilly night air as she left Jake's house, wondering how she'd been so easily outmaneuvered. "Now wait a minute." She paused by the door of her truck to face Colton. "Why do you need a ride home?"

"I rode in with Quinn and Juliet." Colton yanked the passenger door open and slid inside.

"Why couldn't they give you a ride home?" Melanie grumbled as she climbed into her truck.

"They're all kissy-kissy." Colton shut the door. "You look tired. Want me to drive?"

"Sorry, control freak. Enjoy the passenger side." Melanie ignited the engine and decided to enjoy the ride.

"I am not a control freak. I just like to drive."

"Huh." The guy didn't like the wheel in anybody else's hands. Melanie hit a pothole at the end of Jake's drive.

"You did that on purpose," Colton muttered.

"Prove it." Yeah, she'd nailed that one.

"Did you have fun tonight?" Colt asked.

"Yes." She felt right at home with the Lodge-Freeze family and had truly enjoyed playing with both Nathan and Leila. God, she wanted kids. So badly. "How did the board meeting go?"

"Fine. They didn't call for my head—yet anyway."

"They are a patient group." For some reason, needling Colton had become a good goal since he'd been so serious all night. "There's plenty of time. It's not like you use your head much."

He chuckled. "Any reason you're tempting me to toss your ass over my knee again?"

Heat zinged through her body to land between her legs. "Threaten me again, and you'll walk home, Freeze." Her voice remained level, and triumph filled her.

They came upon the ridge overlooking Mineral Lake, and Colton pointed to the overhang, which stood to the side and could see over most of the nearest valley. "Pull over for a sec. I can see the Angus from here."

Melanie pulled over.

Colton grinned before twisting the ignition and taking the keys.

"Hey." Silence surrounded them, and Melanie turned toward him. "Give me the keys."

"You ever park here?" Colt asked, his voice soft, his eyes glowing in the moonlight.

The sexy tone licked over her skin. "No. Give me the keys." This time, her voice wavered.

"Come and get them." He slipped them into his front pocket.

Images of what lay just behind that pocket filled her

mind and heated her body. "You're a little too old for that game," she breathed.

"Ah, baby. You're never too old for that game." He reached down and unbuckled her belt. "You've been pushing me all night. Why don't you just get it out of your system?"

"Meaning, what?"

"You're mad at my reaction to your calling Dawn, and I get that. But I apologized, so let's get past it."

She drew in a deep breath. "You think you're so charming that an apology can get you past anything, don't you?" He had a right to think that, considering his charm had always worked. Plus, he usually meant his words, so his apologies were sincere.

"If words aren't enough, what do you want?" He caressed down her arm to her thigh, and her muscle bunched beneath his firm grasp.

She swallowed. "Nothing. Words are fine."

He leaned closer, his hand sliding to her knee, his breath heating her ear. "I don't think so. What else could I possibly do to make you forgive me?"

Her entire body shuddered as she tried to retain control and not rip his clothes off.

"Seduction is a waste of time." She hoped the words emerged logically.

He chuckled, and the sound vibrated straight to her clit. "We both know you just meant to challenge me."

She had no clue what she'd meant to do, since her mind had pretty much shut down. Her body trembled with a need so great it astounded her. The man had barely touched her. "No challenge intended."

He caressed up her thigh to press against the apex of her

legs. "Open for me, baby."

She grabbed the steering wheel with both hands, the stars blurring high in the sky. "We're in the truck."

"I know." He nipped her ear, and she stopped breathing. Then she slid her knees farther apart.

"Good girl," he breathed, quickly unzipping her jeans and slipping one finger beneath her panties. "So, about our game."

She blinked again, biting her lip to keep from gyrating against his hand. "G-game?"

"Yeah." He licked along the shell of her ear. "The game is called two minutes—over and under."

She shut her eyes and tried to concentrate while the world narrowed to his talented fingers. "I don't know that game." Her words came out in a breathless rush, and she couldn't help rolling her hips.

"It's easy. When I say *go*, I either make you come within two minutes, or I don't. Feel free to fight it." He tugged on her clit for emphasis. "If I win, I choose where we stay the night, and you forgive me. If you win, you can continue being irritated and spend the night by yourself."

Two minutes? She could make it a measly two minutes. "And…I get Feisty's next colt." Feisty was Colt's favored thoroughbred champion, and she should be foaling within the next year.

Colton chuckled. "Fair enough. But if the stakes are that high, you have to keep your hands on the steering wheel and your legs open. You change either of those, and you lose."

"Fine." Drawing on any dignity and pride she could find, she settled her mind to think about taxes next year.

"Are you ready?" he asked, licking down her neck.

God, no. Her skin tingled where he roamed. "Give it

your best shot, Freeze." *Taxes. Numbers. Shoes. Bunions. What the hell was a bunion, anyway?*

"*Go*," he whispered. Then he released her and leaned back.

Her eyelids shot open. "What—"

"Keep your hands on the wheel." He pushed a button on his watch, and then expertly slipped open her blouse buttons. "You. Can't. Move."

Desire ran with heated claws through her abdomen. She could do this. Two minutes. Only two minutes.

He flicked open the front clasp of her bra.

Crap. She should've worn a different bra. A sports bra, even. Wetness coated her thigh, and she fought to keep from rubbing her legs together.

His rough hand palmed one breast, and she bit back a harsh moan.

He reached across her and pulled a lever, sliding the seat back about ten inches.

"No, you—"

He smiled and leaned in to enclose one nipple. "Be quiet, Mel, and hold on to the wheel."

Her knuckles ached as she tightened her hold.

He bit down enough to have her crying out. Electrical shocks cascaded from her nipple to her sex. "God." Her head fell back on the headrest.

Wet and rough, his tongue bathed her smarting flesh. "I love how you respond," he murmured. "Have you ever been tied up?"

A spiraling started deep in her sex, and she fought to concentrate, to hold back the impending orgasm. "No, and it's not going to happen," she panted.

The heel of his palm pressed down on her clit at the same time as he inched two fingers inside her. "I think it will happen," he said, crisscrossing his fingers and zeroing in on her G-spot.

Oh God, Oh God, Oh God. A rushing sound filled her ears, and her body began to gyrate against her will.

He levered up and kissed her, hard and deep. She lost herself in his mouth, in his determination, in the very maleness that was Colton.

She could do this. Kiss him and not come. Except he had two hands.

Without warning, his tongue swept her mouth just as he pushed down on her clit, his free hand tweaking her nipple.

Hard.

She exploded from the inside out, white flashes zipping behind her eyelids. Waves of intense pleasure ripped through her, breasts to toes, undulating her abdomen, making her cry out into his mouth.

His magical fingers prolonged her orgasm, forcing her to ride the waves until her entire body went lax. She flopped back against the leather as he removed his hands and refastened her bra and shirt.

Finally, panting, she opened one eye. "Time?"

Arrogance, amusement, and an alarming gentleness curved his smile as he glanced at his watch. "Eighty-two seconds. I guess you're mine for the entire night."

Her stomach clenched, and her breasts, already at attention, yipped a *yahoo*. God. How in the world was she going to survive an entire night with Colton Freeze?

• • •

Colton nudged his cabin door open, wondering idly if he should carry Melanie inside. Were his brothers right? Was this actually love? The idea was starting to seem plausible and not so alarming.

Melanie stepped inside and grinned. "Colton Freeze, folks. The most organized, well-planned financial genius in town…and complete slob."

He shut the door and grinned. "I'm not a slob." Then he glanced around at his boots by the door, shirts on the couch, and dry groceries he'd failed to put away still sitting on the table. "Maybe?"

She laughed and began folding clean shirts. "You're not dirty, just messy."

"Oh baby, I can be dirty." He wiggled his eyebrows in a way guaranteed to make her laugh harder.

She wiped her eyes. "I love the sound of the stream out back."

"Me too." He liked living to the west of everyone. The one bedroom cabin had one bathroom and a main living space that consisted of a living room, eating nook, and kitchen. A massive stone fireplace took up one wall, and windows another. The stream outside was a constant flow.

Wind rattled pine needles against the window.

He took the shirts from her and tossed them on a chair. "Have you noticed we haven't made love in a bed yet?"

Pink slid across her face, and he watched, fascinated.

His phone buzzed, and only the need to find out about Hawk could pull Colt's attention from Melanie. "Freeze."

"Colt? It's Dad. Hawk has slipped into a coma."

Chapter Eighteen

Melanie left the hospital and drew her coat closer together as the wind tried to chill her bones. When would spring begin to show up? Worry cascaded even more coldness through her.

How could Hawk be in a coma? She'd spent the morning talking to him and trying to get him to awaken, but he hadn't moved. Colton was working on the ranch but would head to the hospital as soon as possible.

Hawk needed to awaken.

She slipped into her truck and drove back to Mineral Lake, stopping in front of Kurt's Koffees to return her shirt. She'd quit her other two town jobs the other day and didn't miss them a bit.

After giving Kurt a hug, she loped next door to the new deli where Dawn already sat in a booth, sipping a soda.

"Hi." Melanie dropped onto the bench, her entire body aching.

"Hi." Dark circles accentuated the hollows beneath Dawn's bloodshot eyes. She'd pulled her dark hair up in a clip and wore jeans with a sweater. "I ordered turkey sandwiches for us both. How was the hospital?"

"He's the same." Melanie signaled for a soda. "Did you stay at the hospital all night?"

"I read a romance novel to him." Dawn's smile barely lifted her lips. "I figured he'd wake up and protest."

Melanie nodded. "That should've done it."

The bell over the door jingled, and Mrs. Joskly, the town librarian for as long as anyone could remember, bustled inside with a hulking blond giant.

"Oh, good. I thought I saw you come in, Melanie. This is my grandson, George, visiting from Boise." Mrs. Joskly straightened her peacoat.

"Ma'am," George said, his deep voice matching his beefy body. Green eyes sparkled out of his round face, giving him the look of the Jolly Green Giant. He gingerly slipped his arm out of Mrs. Joskly's grasp. "I'll go order sandwiches, Naney."

Mrs. Joskly waited until he'd lumbered toward the counter before speaking. "I was hoping you'd show Georgie around town, Melanie."

Melanie glanced toward George's broad back. "He looks about seventeen, Mrs. Joskly."

"Oh no, dear. Georgie is eighteen and perfectly legal. Come on." Mrs. Joskly winked a cataract-laden eye. "We all like to play the cougar once in a while, now don't we?"

Dawn coughed into her water glass.

Melanie tried to keep from wincing. "How long will Georgie be in town, ma'am?"

"Just until next Tuesday," Mrs. Joskly said cheerfully, clapping her mittens together. "Then you'll have to say good-bye forever."

Dawn cleared her throat. "Is Tuesday the day you have for the town pool, Mrs. Joskly?"

"Of course not." The librarian gave her patented hard stare down her nose. "I have the following week. I certainly don't expect a good girl like Melanie to date George on Tuesday and declare her love on Wednesday for Colton. That should take a least a week."

Melanie leaned back when the waitress delivered their sandwiches. "I appreciate the offer, but I'm busy with work. Plus, I'm sure Georgie would have more fun hanging out with kids his own age."

Mrs. Joskly sighed heavily. "Well, I suppose so. But keep two weeks from Thursday in mind, would you?"

"Of course." Melanie smiled weakly and reached for her sandwich.

Dawn waited until Mrs. Joskly had joined her grandson across the deli. "This bet is getting odd, right?"

"Very. Any idea who the bet taker is?" Melanie asked.

Dawn frowned. "I really don't know, but I've been out of town at school, so that's not surprising." She took a bite of sandwich and chewed thoughtfully for a moment. "Did you ask me to lunch to talk or *to talk*?"

"I asked you to lunch to chat and not about Hawk, not about Colton, and certainly not about love." Melanie sipped her soda.

"Perfect." Dawn sighed, relief crossing her classic features. "I don't have the energy for a real heart-to-heart."

"Me either. So tell me about your classes." Melanie

snagged a chip from her plate.

They finished their lunches, and right about as Melanie finished her chips, a twinge from the ride side of her abdomen caught her attention. She sat back and took a deep breath. Another twinge. Damn it.

"Excuse me," she said to Dawn and then slipped from the booth, heading toward the restroom. A quick glance in the one stall confirmed another shattered dream.

She'd started her period.

Her mind swam, and traitorous tears pricked the back of her eyes. Sure, it was foolish. But she'd believed, deep down, since Colton wanted to get her pregnant, that it'd work.

Hurt washed through her along with the rest of her hope.

A five percent chance was no chance at all, especially since that five percent might now be gone.

Her mind clicked to moments of Colton holding little Nathan, of him taking Leila on a date. The man loved kids and certainly wanted his own. Why wouldn't he? The Freeze genes were pretty damn good.

Logically, she knew this wasn't her fault. But deep down, in a place she hated to visit, shame lived. She couldn't have kids. She'd never feel the beginning of a life, of being kicked in the tummy, of sharing a body.

That awareness brought physical pain.

She knew Colton as well as she knew herself. He'd stick with her, no matter what, especially if she needed him. But what about his dreams? Plus, it wasn't like he'd declared any love.

They had friendship, they had trust. Hell, maybe he did love her. The kind of love that came from childhood, that came from genuine friendship.

If it had been the happily-ever-after forever kind, he would've said so.

Sometimes silence hurt worse than the most hateful of words.

She took a deep breath and left the restroom, already planning her future alone.

Dawn glanced up. "Are you okay? You're pale."

"I'm fine." Melanie placed bills on the table. "Just a little headache. Let's get back to the hospital and force Hawk to wake up." Then she'd plan her life alone.

· · ·

Colton stood outside Hawk's hospital room, trying to keep from punching the doctor in the face. "What do you mean, his vitals are slowing?"

The doctor sighed. "The brain is a mystery, and the longer he's in a coma, the less likely he'll awaken. We'd like to helicopter him to Seattle."

"When he wakes up, he'll want to be home." Reality began to spin away.

The doctor nodded. "I understand. But I also think you should prepare yourself for the possibility that he's not waking up."

"No." Colton pivoted on his heel and went into the room to drop into a chair. The quiet silence was filled with the scents of bleach and plastic.

He stretched back in the plastic hospital chair, his gaze on his buddy. The person he'd always told everything to, the person who had his back no matter what.

Hawk lay in the bed, not moving. Although his skin

showed his Native American heritage, he looked pale. Wounded. Hurting.

Colton glanced down at his muddied jeans. Mud, snow, and blood.

Despair hunched his shoulders. Life was out of control, and he hated it. The idea of losing Hawk burned like acid in his gut. He had to fix everything somehow. "I'm not leaving this seat until you fucking wake up," he whispered to his silent friend.

And he wouldn't. A promise was a promise.

A rustle sounded by the door, and his dad slipped inside. He walked toward the bed, examined the beeping machines, and rested a large-boned hand on Hawk's forehead. "How is our boy doing?"

Colton wiped his eyes. "His vitals have slowed, which is bad."

Tom nodded and turned to take the next chair. "I made Dawn go home and get some sleep."

"I think only one of us is supposed to be in here." Colt said woodenly.

Tom extended long legs and crossed his boots at the ankles. "I'd like to see them bodily remove us."

Colton studied his dad. Although in his mid-fifties, Tom looked much younger. Broad across the shoulders, tall, and in excellent shape. He had the same blue eyes as Colton and Dawn. "Good point," Colton said.

Tom glanced down at the bloody jeans and then up at Colton's face. "Cattle kicked you?"

"Yes. The other day."

"At Mel's house?" Tom asked.

"Yes. When I stayed over." Colton had always leveled

with his dad, and he wouldn't stop now.

Tom scratched his strong jaw. "I wondered if you two would ever get together."

"Me too. But now I'm not sure we'll ever be friends again. If I screw this up, too."

"So don't screw it up." Tom shot him a look. "Do you want things to go back the way they were?"

"No." The word emerged before Colt even had to think about it. "I don't want to just be her friend. She's pretty much everything." At the thought of losing her, of not having her as a constant in his life, his gut clenched. Even more so, the thought of her loving somebody else made him want to hit the wall.

Tom nodded. "Been there. Your mother was a friend before we got together. In fact, her husband was my best friend. When he died, we both felt lost."

Colton straightened and glanced at his dad. "I never really thought about that. Must've been tough."

"It was." His dad sighed, stretching out farther. "At first, we just helped each other cope. Jake was so confused, and Quinn was so angry, we concentrated on them. Then, one day I turned around, and bam."

Yeah. *Bam.* Colt exhaled.

Tom cleared his throat. "It's nice to see you struggle a little."

"What?" Colton pivoted to face his dad.

Tom flashed a dimple. "You've always had girls and now women flocking toward you." He snorted. "No doubt because you inherited my good looks and charm."

Colton rolled his eyes. "Right."

"Okay. Your mama's good looks and charm." Tom cast

a worried glance at Hawk. "Mel knows you, and she knows your bullshit. She also won't put up with it."

Colton frowned. "What's your point?"

"You eased into a relationship with no risk, and I bet you haven't even told her how you really feel." Thoughtful contemplation, not judgment, echoed in Tom's low tone.

Shit, had he? Colton rubbed his chin. "I wanted to get my feet under me first."

Tom shook his head. "There's no getting your feet under you when you love a woman the way we do. Just hope you don't land on your face when you fall." He turned to pin his son with a hard look. "But make sure you mean it, because if you hurt that girl, I'll kick your ass myself."

"Fair enough." Colton glanced down at his demolished jeans. "I should probably clean up first."

"If you two are done with your hen fest, I'd like to get some rest," Hawk rasped from the bed.

Colt and Tom immediately launched themselves toward the bed.

"Hawk?" Colton asked, his voice shaking.

Hawk glared up through bloodshot eyes. "Stop hovering. You two block out the light."

"I'll get a doctor." Tom hustled from the room.

Colton smiled down at his buddy. "You're all right."

• • •

Melanie slipped off her gloves as she hurried down the hallway to Hawk's room, where a small celebration had taken over. The Lodge boys and their wives took up one wall, while Tom and Dawn sat in the chairs. Colton leaned against the wall by the head of the bed, and she studiously ignored him.

"Hey, Mel," Hawk said, his voice hoarse. He was sitting up, propped against a couple of pillows.

Relief swept through her so quickly her knees trembled. "It's about time you stopped napping," she said, striding toward the bed to get a better look.

His green eyes were clear, and while bandages covered a good part of him, he looked alert. "I'm fine. Stop frowning."

She schooled her face into calm lines. "How's the head?" Reaching out, she smoothed his dark hair away from his broad face. The purple bruise across his temple had faded to a striated red.

"Fine." He glanced at the clock near the far wall. "I'm leaving in a few minutes, probably."

"No, you're not." Loni Freeze swept into the room with a Crock-Pot in her hands. "I brought you soup."

Dawn laughed. "Mom, they have food here."

"Not as good as mine." Loni set the pot on the counter and tugged a bowl from her massive handbag. Her dark hair had been braided down her back, and she wore a pretty purple blouse with a wool skirt. "Chicken noodle has healing properties." Ignoring the amusement around her, she ladled a healthy portion into the bowl and handed it to Hawk. "Eat."

"Yes, ma'am," he said, accepting the spoon.

Melanie kept her gaze on Hawk, although she could feel Colton's on her. Yeah, he knew her well enough to understand something was on her mind. Maybe he wanted for her to end things so he didn't have to do so.

The guy should take the easy out and run.

The doctor entered the room, his weary gray gaze taking in the entire group. "What happened to the limit on visitors we set?"

Hawk blew on his spoon.

"When can he come home?" Loni asked, looking almost miniature next to Colton.

Hawk paused. "To my house."

"No, sweetie. To ours." Loni bent and tucked Hawk more firmly in. "You shouldn't be on your own for a while. Just until we make sure your brain is working all right."

Colton and his brothers all stiffened in an obvious attempt to prevent jumping at the easy one-liner.

Melanie smirked. None of them were brave enough to tick off Loni.

Hawk blinked twice, raw emotion crossing his face to be quickly vanquished.

Loni ignored his struggle for control and pressed a motherly kiss to his forehead. "You're family, and you're not getting out of my sight until I make sure you're all right."

Now a slight panic lifted Hawk's eyebrow.

"Melanie and I can take care of Hawk at Mel's house," Colton said calmly.

Mel's gaze slashed to meet his, which was full of challenge. He hadn't. He really hadn't.

Loni clasped her hands together. "Well, Mel's is closer to Hawk's spread so he can keep an eye on things. Colton's cabin isn't big enough, and I can visit Mel's house daily. Yes, that's a good plan."

The other men in the room were suddenly busy looking elsewhere. Anywhere but at Mel.

Oh, she knew a good setup when one smacked her over

the head. "I'd be thrilled to have you stay with me, Hawk. Loni, you're welcome any time and any day. Colton, you don't live with me."

Hawk glanced from Colton to Melanie. "What did I miss?" he asked slowly.

"Nothing," Melanie answered just as Colton said, "A lot."

Anger slid through her veins like Pop Rocks. How dare he put her on the spot like this? Some privacy would be nice.

The doctor coughed. "It's time for a new MRI for Hawk. I'm going to have to ask you all to leave."

Melanie winked at Hawk. "I'll be back later, and we'll plan your getaway."

He grinned and handed his bowl back to Loni. "That's a plan."

With a hard look at Colton, she turned and exited the room, her boots echoing on the hard tiles as she hurried down the hallway and out into the sunny day.

Weak but bright, the sun glimmered off the frosty ground and myriad of vehicles scattered around the parking lot.

She almost made it to her truck before Colton swung her around.

Jerking her arm away, she allowed her temper to blow. "What the hell do you think you're doing?"

He frowned, amusement glinting in his blue eyes. "You don't want to help Hawk?"

Exasperation melded with anger. "Of course I want to help him. But I don't need you offering for me, and I sure as hell don't need you making some sort of announcement that we're living together. We're not." In fact, they were breaking up. "It's over." She took a deep breath and tried to keep her face calm. "We're over, Colton."

"What if you're pregnant?" he asked softly.

The tears ignored her and filled her eyes. "I'm not. I've already started and will very soon end my period." One of the dubious benefits of her condition—very short periods, sometimes only lasting a day or two.

"Oh." He exhaled heavily. "So we'll try again."

"No. This is too much, and it's too complicated. We started because of the urgency, and now it's too late. We're just friends pretending to be more, Colton." At least, he was. Unless he disagreed?

He blinked and shook his head. "Mel—"

Her chin lifted. "Back off, Freeze. Whatever we had, it's over. Deal with it."

The slow smile he gave her tingled awareness along her skin, through her breasts, between her legs. "Ah, Mel." He stepped into her space, and her butt hit her door. "Please tell me you meant that as a challenge."

She kept her gaze steady. "I meant that as a brush-off, you arrogant ass."

"Prove it." He settled both hands on the truck, caging her.

"More games?" She tried for sarcasm, but her voice emerged breathy.

He leaned in, his lips brushing her temple. "Last time we played a game, you screamed my name as you came. Wanna play again?"

Lava flowed down her back. "You're boring me." Okay. She may have meant that one as a challenge.

He lifted away, his gaze hot. "Am I, now? Well, let's test that theory with one kiss. I'll kiss you, and if you don't respond, then I'll walk away and believe you're done with me."

"Colt—"

"Afraid?" he taunted.

Stubborn pride straightened her spine. "No. Kiss away, and when you lose, keep your lips to yourself."

"That would be a true pity considering how much my lips love every dip and crevice in your body."

Those crevices began to ache. "Hurry up."

He leaned back in. "Fine." Without warning, his hand fisted in her hair and tugged. The erotic move shot arousal straight to her core. Her neck elongated, and her chest lifted against his torso. His toned body brushed against her in blatant masculinity.

She swallowed and tried to keep her eyelids from dropping. Her hands clenched into fists to keep from grabbing him.

He twisted his wrist, angling her face.

Colt had a way of overwhelming her, making her feel feminine. That appealing warmth competed heavily with her sense of self preservation.

His lips hovered an inch from hers.

She breathed out, trying not to move.

He flicked out his tongue, licking the corner of her mouth. She shuddered, her breasts scraping his chest. She felt his smile as his mouth slid against hers.

Gentle, sweet, and firm, he kissed her as if they had all day. Slow and drugging, he took his time, his body heating hers, so much bigger and stronger. An edge lived in Colton Freeze, always had, but this was the first time she'd felt its bite.

He increased his pressure until she opened her mouth.

Then he swept inside, staking a claim.

He took her under, he took her over, Colt in full force.

She'd underestimated him.

The hand in her hair tightened, holding her in place. Where he wanted her.

Her eyelids fluttered shut and she fell into the storm, kissing him back, her tongue mating with his.

He growled deep, his free hand clasping the back of her thigh and lifting. His cock pulsed between her legs, and she struggled to get closer. To feel more.

She protested when he broke the kiss and lifted his head. Then she gasped.

Hunger glittered in his sky-dark eyes, crimson spiraled across his pronounced cheekbones. His nostrils flared much like a stallion's as it hunted a mate. The boy she'd known was gone.

Only a fully grown, dangerous man held her tight.

Need flushed through her. Every nerve she owned screamed for release. Her knees trembled, and her sex ached for him.

He released her hair and leg, tugging her way from the truck so he could open her door. His hands encircled her waist, and he lifted her into the seat. Then he shut the door and turned to walk away.

Without saying a word.

Chapter Nineteen

That night, Colton wanted to kick himself as he strode into the hospital, its bright lights cutting through the dark hour. He'd worked on accounts all day, trying to make up for the shortfall from Mark's deception.

He'd sucked at it all day, because his mind had been elsewhere.

On a pretty brunette who'd pretty much blown his world apart with one little kiss in the parking lot.

He'd almost gotten down on one knee and proposed right then and there—after she'd dumped him. What the hell was wrong with him?

Sure, he cared for her. Hell, he loved her. But it didn't have to throw him into a tailspin like this. She'd been correct when she'd called him a control freak. He'd always liked things just so.

Melanie was blowing his *just so* to hell.

He had to get a grip on himself, and then proceed

accordingly. First, they would start dating again without any more crap about breaking up. Then, they'd slowly make sure they were right for each other, which of course they were, and then in a year or two, he'd propose.

If she became pregnant in the meantime, the timeline would adjust.

Now that plan worked.

Feeling much better, he strode into the hospital and stopped short at the barracuda manning the receiving counter. A hodgepodge of wrinkles cascaded around brightly painted red lips formed in a scowl. "Visiting hours are over," she said in a deep voice.

He dawned his most charming smile. "My friend texted me to come down and keep him company. I promise I'll be quiet."

"No." She stood and crossed impressive arms. "Visiting hours begin tomorrow at nine in the morning. Come back then."

He scratched his head. "Could I just poke my head in and tell him I'll be back tomorrow?"

"No. Leave or I'll call security."

Wow. "Have a nice day, ma'am." He turned and stalked outside, hiding his grin. Then he loped toward his truck, dialing Hawk's number.

"Where are you?" his friend growled.

"Blocked by a wild one in receiving. I'll come back tomorrow." Colton reached his door.

"I'm leaving tonight. Come by the window." Something crashed in the background.

Colt's head jerked up. "You're not okay to leave."

"Yet, I'm leaving."

Damn it. "Stay in bed. I'll be right there." Colton eyed the building and jogged around the manicured lawn to the north. "Flick your lights."

Instead of flicking, Hawk slid open a window.

Colton scaled an overgrown shrub and two hydrangeas to grab the snowy sill and haul himself inside the room. The scent of bleach and plastic smashed into his senses. All of a sudden, they were wild teenagers again. He grinned at his buddy. "What the hell?"

Hawk stood on the other side of the bed, still in a hospital gown, his white cast almost glowing. "Tell me you brought clothes."

"No. You haven't been released."

Hawk scratched the scruff along his jaw. "I can't stay here another minute."

The guy had just awakened from a coma. "Listen, I know it's tough. But you really should stay here another few days." If he had to call Loni, he would.

"No." Hawk padded barefoot for the door. "Let's go."

Colton snorted. "The woman at the front will probably call security to stop you…at least until the doctor shows up and gets all those forms you have to sign if you're leaving against medical orders."

Hawk paused and turned around. "I hadn't thought of that."

Relief had Colton nodding. "So you might as well get back into bed and wait for the doctor to do his rounds tomorrow morning."

Hawk eyed the window. "I have another idea."

Shit. Colton shook his head, trying to reason with his buddy. "No, no, no. That's a bad idea."

Hawk shrugged and lifted a leg over the icy sill, exposing his ass.

God. Colton blinked. "Now I have to burn out my eyeballs."

Hawk threw him a hard look. "Are you going to help or not?"

Colton sighed. "Your mind is made up?"

"I'm heading out of here with or without your help." Hawk winced as he tried to scoot across the sill with bare legs.

"Fine." Colton pulled him back. "Take my boots."

"No. Just hurry the hell up." Hawk glanced at the empty doorway.

Colton shook his head. "Let me go first." He nimbly jumped back outside the window. "Okay, come on out." He prepared to catch his oldest friend.

Hawk gingerly slid both legs out, hampered by the broken arm.

The sill cracked.

Their gazes met in alarm a split second before wood splintered, and Hawk went flying.

Colton reached up as Hawk pummeled into him, sending them both sprawling into the nearest hydrangea. Dead, snow-covered leaves crashed against Colt's back, and Hawk's front.

Hawk yelped and rolled over.

Colton sat up. "Is your skull okay?"

"My brain is the least of my worries," Hawk hissed, yanking a rough branch from his groin.

"My eyes," Colton muttered, wiping a forearm across them. "Stop fucking flashing me."

"Jealous?" Hawk snorted and then winced again.

No, but he was starting to feel like a dumbass. Colton stood and yanked Hawk to his feet. "Let's get out of here before they call security."

Hawk nodded and brushed dirt and ice from his hospital gown.

Colton bit down on his lip. Hard.

His best buddy stood, legs bare, hospital gown flapping in the wind. A bunch of leaves twisted in Hawk's hair, and dirt smudged his battered cheek. "What?"

Laughter rolled up inside Colton, and he let it loose.

"Shut up." Hawk finally cracked a smile and then snorted.

Lights flipped on in the room behind them. They both stilled.

"Run," Hawk hissed.

Colton nodded and helped Hawk over the shrubs, laughing and trying not to fall. They hitched along, Hawk's ass flashing, until breaking into a clumsy jog and reaching Colt's truck.

They jumped inside, and Colt ignited the engine. He turned to survey Hawk. "Are you sure you're well enough to leave?"

"Positive. Now *go*." Hawk flipped on the heat and shoved his reddened feet toward the blast of air.

With one more chuckle, Colton threw the truck in drive and escaped the security now pouring out of the front entrance. "Did we just break any laws?"

"Dunno." Hawk exhaled. "But it's good to be alive, right?"

"Damn straight." Colton grinned. "When are you going to tell me who beat the hell out of you?"

Hawk stiffened and then lifted a shoulder. "I'm not. It's

over, and he looks worse than I do."

"Promise?"

"Yes."

"If you needed help, you'd ask?" Colton kept his gaze on the road.

"You're the only person I'd ask, and I promise I would." Hawk leaned his head back.

Colton nodded. Good enough. His buddy was now on the mend. Time to settle things with Melanie.

• • •

The quiet rapping on the door had Melanie padding in her fuzzy socks and peering out the window. The fire in the hearth crackled happily behind her. What in the world?

Yanking open the door, she could only gape. "Brian?"

Brian Milton stood on her porch wearing board shorts, a tank top, and an opened parka. In zero degree weather, he was wearing shorts? His hair was mussed, and he'd allowed a shadow to darken his jaw. "I'm taking your advice and moving to Maui." He brushed by her into the warm living room. "I know it's late to call on you, but I want you to come with me."

Her mouth opened and closed. She shook her head. "It's only ten at night, and you're always welcome to visit. You want me to go to Maui?"

"Yes." He pushed the door shut behind her. "A friend of mine from school owns a surf shop, and I bought in yesterday. Come with me, Mel. Leave the cold of Montana and let's live on the beach."

She shoved unruly hair away from her face. "We broke

up, Brian."

He showed a charming dimple. "I know. Come as my friend. For now."

"Huh?"

"I don't know. Perhaps our friendship could turn into more in a different environment. One where we relax and live by the sun." He ran a finger down the side of her face. "A new start for us both."

The touch didn't do a darn thing for her. She stepped back. "I appreciate the offer, but I don't think so."

"Come on." His brown eyes sparkled. "Why stay here, anyway?"

For the first time, the idea of leaving tempted her. Well, depending where she and Colton stood. First, she had to figure a few things out.

"How did your mom take the new plan?" Melanie asked.

Brian winced. "Not well. But my brothers supported me, and I'm sure Mother will come around. Now how about you?"

She smiled. "I don't think so. But who knows, maybe I'll visit for a vacation."

Brian sighed. "Okay. But promise if you want to get out of Montana sometime this spring you'll give me a call." He leaned in and captured her in a big hug. "I don't know if I'd be making this move if you hadn't encouraged me." His lips smacked her.

The door shot open, and Colton stood there supporting Hawk's weight.

Sparks lit Colton's eyes. He pushed Hawk against the wall and rushed Brian, jerking him away from Melanie.

"Wait—" Melanie started.

Colton shoved Brian against the wall. "What the hell?"

"Lighten up, dude." Brian's eyes bugged out.

Anger roared through Melanie. "Let him go, Colton." She dashed toward him and yanked on his arm. Impressive muscles vibrated beneath her palm. "Now."

Colton leaned his face closer to Brian's. "Why was your mouth on hers?"

"Stop being a freakin' jackass." She pulled but wasn't strong enough to budge him. She looked for help from Hawk, but he was leaning against the wall and taking deep breaths.

"Fine." Colt released Brian. "Leave."

"I am." Brian gave her a quick nod. "I'm not leaving for Maui until tomorrow morning. Give me a call if you want to come." He sauntered to the door and let himself out.

Melanie rounded on Colton. "What in the fiery pits of hell is wrong with you?" she yelled.

"With me?" he shouted back. "I get here, and you're kissing Milton? *Milton?*"

"Who I kiss is my business, not yours." If she got any madder, she just might kick him in the face.

"Uh, guys?" Hawk asked.

"Just a second," Colton and Melanie said in unison.

Colton stepped toward her. "You are not going to Maui with that moron."

She lifted her chin, both hands going to her waist. "I'll go anywhere I darn well please, with anybody I want. You can suck it."

"Guys?" Hawk asked.

"Suck what?" Colton said, his face calming. "You name it, I will."

He was such an ass. Melanie rolled her eyes. "Get out of my house."

"Not a chance."

She saw red and swung.

He easily stepped back. "I taught you to fight better than that, chickie. Try again."

Fire lanced through her. She faked a punch and kicked him squarely in the gut. The impact ricocheted up her leg. Holy ouch.

He grinned, not seeming the bit fazed. "Much better."

"Guys!" Hawk bellowed.

"What?!?" They both turned toward him as he slid down the wall to land on his ass.

Oh crap. Melanie rushed toward him, colliding with Colton. They went down in a tangle of arms and legs. Her elbow thumped on the floor, zinging pain through her arm. Ouch.

"Wait." Colton settled her on the floor and regained his balance. "Hawk? Are you all right?"

Hawk leaned against the wall, his face pale, his eyes shut. "No."

"Why in the world did you take him from the hospital?" Melanie hissed, grabbing Hawk's good hand and holding tight.

"We thought it a good idea at the time." Colton shoved to his feet and helped Melanie up. "Grab his other arm." Reaching down, he hauled Hawk up. "Do we need to go back to the hospital?"

"No. I just need sleep." Hawk swayed and leaned heavily on Colton. "Bed."

Melanie nodded toward the guest room past the kitchen.

"Let's take him in there." They slowly maneuvered their buddy into bed, and Melanie judiciously decided not to inform Hawk she'd seen his butt. Once he was all tucked in, he fell asleep within a minute.

Colton inhaled, his gaze on his wounded friend. "I'll have Doc Mooncaller drop by first thing tomorrow morning to check on him."

"Okay," Melanie whispered, shutting off the light and leaving the room.

Colton quietly shut the door. "Do you want to continue our fight?"

"No." Every bone she owned wanted to sleep. "How about we put the fight on hold and take turns watching Hawk tonight? He shouldn't be out of the hospital."

Colton's eyes warmed. "It's a deal. Why don't you get some sleep, and I'll take first watch here on the couch."

Melanie rubbed her nose. "Say check on him every half an hour?"

"Yes. Night, Mel."

"Night." She tiptoed up the stairs to her room, although Hawk had fallen into a deep sleep. Once under the covers, she glanced at her moonlit room. Tons of pictures of she, Colt, and Hawk decorated the vanity that matched her antique bedroom set.

They'd been through so much together through the years. She counted sheep for a while, and then she counted imaginary dragons. The sexiest man she'd ever met sat just a floor beneath her.

A man who knew how to kiss. *Really* knew how to kiss.

Warmth heated through her, and she shifted restlessly.

Finally, a couple of hours after going to bed, she threw

back the covers. Might as well check on Hawk since she couldn't sleep. She trumped down the stairs and glanced into the living room.

Colton sat on the sofa, legs extended onto the coffee table, the firelight dancing over the hard angles of his face. His eyes were closed.

She tiptoed into Hawk's room, her shoulders relaxing at his rhythmic breathing. Good.

Then she left the room and crossed into the living area to grab a blanket to spread over Colton. Although the fire still crackled, the temperature had fallen along with the night.

Just as she dropped the blanket on him, he reached out and grabbed her arm. She tumbled onto him. His mouth covered hers in a deep kiss. She kissed him back for all of two seconds, beyond tempted to fall into his heat.

Instead, she pushed against his chest with both hands. "We need to talk."

"After." He licked along her lips, and fire slammed right into her blood. "First, let's try to make it to a bed. Just once."

She wanted this night. Life was too crazy. "Then we talk."

"Yeah." He kissed her, lifting her and carrying her up the stairs, his mouth never stopping. Never letting her take a breath or find a thought.

As lava poured through her veins, she gave up thinking. Later.

For now, all that existed was Colton Freeze and his dangerous mouth.

He set her down on the bed, gently lifted her top and yoga pants off. Sure hands unbuckled his belt, and his clothes joined hers on the floor.

She swallowed, her lids half-dropping. "You have an

amazing body." Gingerly, she slid her fingers along his ripped abs.

"So do you." He flattened his hand across her upper chest and pushed her back, covering her with heat and male. "God...Melanie." His mouth kissed, tasted, and licked her neck, warm breath chasing over her. "You smell so good... all woman."

His scent of wild forest washed over her, through her.

She was practically panting, needed him so much it physically hurt. Her hands wrapped around his shoulders as his knee nudged her legs apart.

She was so ready.

But he took his time, his mouth wandering down her neck, his teeth providing bite. Proof that his gentleness, while seductive, could disappear in a second. He nipped a breast, and she cried out.

"You have no idea how many times I've imagined you, open to me." He laved the other nipple. "How fucking amazing you feel beneath me." His talented fingers found her, pushing deep inside.

Wild shock filled her, and she arched against his hand, her hips tipping.

With a grin, he fucked her with his fingers, his other hand teasing her nipples. Thank goodness her period had ended so quickly, or she wouldn't be so damn comfortable right now. Shock wandered through her at her own boldness while she rocked her hips into his fingers, but one look at his face filled her with confidence.

Gone was the cool, meticulous man. He was transformed into a hungry, primal being, teeth bared, eyes glinting, the sharp edges of his cheekbones flushed with need.

For her. Only for her. "Now, Colton. Please."

His dark blue gaze captured her. She wanted to look away, to protect herself. But as he pressed the head of his cock against her sex, she was trapped.

She spread her knees wider for his hips. He stretched her.

When he was as deep as he could get, he paused and lowered his forehead to hers. He watched her carefully, and she couldn't hide her emotions. Not this time, and not from him.

He slid out and then back in, capturing her hands and pressing them to the bedspread above her head. Taking control, as only Colton could. Steadily, with determination, he began to pound until the only sound in existence was flesh slapping against flesh.

Lava flowed through her blood. Nerves fired throughout her entire body.

His teeth sank into her earlobe. "Come for me. *Now*."

She exploded, coming hard and fast, sobbing his name. The waves battered her, taking her over.

Her eyelids flew open in time to see him fall over the edge. The tendons strained in his neck, and his entire body went rigid.

God, he was beautiful.

Finally, he relaxed against her, his heart beating against her breasts.

She smiled. "Colton—"

"Colton, we can't keep doing this. It's going to rip my heart to shreds. I need you as a friend, not as one of your flings. We know how those end," Mel said.

"Mel, you don't know what you're talking–"

A bang from downstairs startled them both. Colton lifted up and then withdrew from her body. She groaned at the erotic sensations.

"Stay here," he said as he yanked on his jeans and padded from the room.

A clamoring came from Hawk's room.

Melanie jumped up, threw on her bathrobe, and ran down the stairs after Colt, stopping short at the doorway, her heart slamming against her ribs.

Hawk had thrown the lamp across the room, and was struggling out of his blankets while standing. His eyes were open but unseeing, and muscles rippled in his arms as he fought the sheet.

She started toward him, only to have Colton grab her out of the way. "He's not awake." Colton blocked her with his body. "Hawk? Wake up, buddy."

Hawk stilled, and reality slowly dawned across his face. He frowned.

"You had a bad dream," Colton said, stepping forward to tug the constricting blanket from around Hawk's torso. "Sit down. It's time to talk."

With a nod, Hawk dropped back the bed.

Melanie looked from one to the other, her mind spinning. Instinct took over, and she listened. Hawk needed to talk to Colton right now. The both of them would be too much. "I'll see you guys in the morning," she whispered as she shut the door.

She'd finish *her* talk with Colton in the morning.

Chapter Twenty

Colton left the coffeepot on and slipped out of Melanie's house. He needed a shave but didn't have time. In fact, if this was going to work, he had to get a move on.

Hawk hadn't wanted to talk during the night, and Colton didn't feel like pushing him, so they'd played poker. As of five in the morning, Hawk owed Colton two horses and a head of cattle.

Colton grinned. Sure, Hawk would probably win them back the next time they played. Maybe.

They'd spent the night reminiscing and planning. Planning big. But this plan would work. For so long, Colton had lived according to plans, and look where it had gotten him. Sometimes a guy just had to take a chance.

When it mattered.

Hawk had fallen asleep around six, and after Colton checked in on a sleeping Melanie, he made coffee and headed outside. He loved her. Not in the happy, singing, making-out-in-daisies way, but in a his-heart-would-be-ripped-out-with-sharp-claws-if-she-left-him way.

He was about to take the biggest risk of his life, and he couldn't be happier.

Well, or more nauseated. What if this backfired?

With a shrug, he propelled himself full-bore ahead, as he always had. If he was going to crash and burn, there was going to be a hell of a fire.

He pressed speed dial on his phone. "Jake? I need to talk to Leila. Yes. Now." He waited until his niece came on the phone, and then he asked for the help he needed.

With a happy squeal, Leila agreed to help.

He hung up and frowned. They'd need more than the two of them to make this happen. Well, one of the benefits of belonging to a big family was…lots of hands. So he lowered his head and started to make phone calls.

• • •

Melanie stomped her freezing feet on the hard pavement just as snow began to drift down from the sky. "I told you it would snow again today. Now can we go?" she asked her too-silent companion.

"No." Hawk reached over and yanked her coat zipper up with his healthy hand. "It's almost spring. You love the parade."

"Do not—and spring can't show up soon enough." She hadn't gotten enough sleep, her head hurt, and her heart kind of ached. Colton had left without waking her up and finishing their talk. That meant he didn't want to talk, and that pretty much said it all.

Hawk hunched his shoulders against the breeze. "I gave you two cups of coffee and cooked you scrambled eggs with extra cheese. Stop complaining."

Melanie squinted up at her slightly cranky friend. "You'll make some woman a fine wife someday."

He grinned as the little Bluebird troop of five-year-olds sashayed down Main Street. "Thanks."

Melanie glanced behind herself at the warmth all but vibrating from Kurt's Koffees. The aroma of freshly baked orange rolls wafted out when a customer exited the coffee shop. "I think I'll go inside for a bit."

"Stay with me. I'm dizzy." Hawk sounded more amused than dizzy.

She shook her head. "You are not." Then she peered closer at his calm face. "Are you?"

He sighed. "No. But just stay here for a minute, will you? Trust me."

"Fine." She blew on her mitten-covered hands and smiled as the mayor drove by in his vintage 1920 Model T. The Lady Elks were next, then the Boy Scout troops, then the high school cheerleaders, and the high school band.

Candy flew from many hands, and she happily caught a couple of toffees. She unrolled an orange one. "Are you all right? I mean, with the nightmare and everything?"

"I'm fine. My head is better, and I'm sure the nightmares will go away." He craned his neck to look down the parade route.

In other words, no more talking about it. Melanie sighed. "You're a pain, Hawk."

"I know." He nudged her closer to the curb.

She shoved a toffee into her mouth and protested. Then

loud music and flashing lights from down the way caught her attention.

A murmuring settled throughout the crowd lining the streets.

Melanie stood up on her tiptoes to get a better look. A couple of floats, one featuring vampires, and the other the Flintstones, moved along the route, blocking her view of the noisemaker.

A snowflake landed on her nose, and she flicked it off, chewing thoughtfully.

The music was loud enough she could feel the beat beneath her boots. She tapped along, staring to hum.

She grinned. "Hey. It's 'You're the One That I Want.'" She laughed, glancing around. "Where's Colton? He should be here so I can bug him singing." Humming, she tried to lean forward to see the float.

All of a sudden, fireworks exploded up into the air. The float came into view with an electric heart and two huge four-leaf clovers spinning above it, and words strung along the outside but not lit up. She squinted to read the words as Colton stepped up in full 1950s greaser leather jacket and jeans…with a microphone.

She stepped back.

Then, microphone in hand, he started to bellow out the song.

Horribly. Truly horribly.

Neon flashed, and the lights along the side lit up with a *Marry Me, Melanie.*

She shook her head, reality disappearing. *Marry Me?*

Colton jumped down, walking toward her, singing. Kind of.

Leila, Loni, and Dawn hustled behind him, their choruses kind of saving the song.

Melanie's entire body flushed hot.

"Good Lord, his voice is horrible." Hawk coughed out laughter.

"Ah." Melanie's heart jumped hard. Even so, she searched for an escape. People beamed at her from all around.

Colton reached her and stopped singing. "I'm making a declaration."

The crowed whooped around them. Melanie, her mind spinning, wondered idly who'd won the bet.

She shook her head. "Colton—"

"I love you, Mel." He brushed a kiss on her nose. "I don't care about my life plan, I don't care about a schedule…I only care about you. Here and now."

Tears pricked the back of her eyes. God, she wanted him. "I can't have kids." Even so, she dug her fingers into the lapels of the jacket. "I know you want kids."

"I knew that was the holdup with you dropping to a knee and proposing." He shook his head.

"Dropping to a knee?" she asked. Was he kidding?

His gaze ran over her face in a warm caress. "I would adore a spunky miniature brunette baby with eyes like chocolate." He sobered. "But it's a *we* situation. Either *we* can have kids, or *we* can't. If not, we'll adopt. But our lives start with a *we*."

She took a deep breath. Everything she ever wanted stood in front of her in a weathered leather jacket and cocky smile. She knew him, and she'd loved him forever. How in the world could she turn away from such happiness? God, she wanted a life with him. "I love you, too. Marry me?"

He whooped and picked her up, swinging her around. "I thought you'd never ask. Yes." Then he slipped an antique diamond ring on her finger. "It was my grandmother's."

The crowd erupted in cheers.

Colton kissed her deep, emotion in every line of his hard body. Finally, he lifted his head and looked around, keeping a tight hold on Melanie. "Well? Who won?"

Everyone glanced around. Finally, Loni stepped forward, her face turning a very pretty pink. "Ah, Mrs. Hudson and I did. We went in halfsies."

Mrs. Hudson danced across the street, her wool coat flapping beneath a knitted florescent orange scarf. "Whoo hoo! You were right, Loni. You do know your boy."

Colton's mouth dropped open. "Mom?"

Tom jumped out of the driver's seat of the float. "Loni Eleanor Freeze? You did not bet on this."

Loni laughed. "You're just mad I won and you didn't."

Tom scratched his chin and threw an arm around his wife. "I had tomorrow as my date."

Melanie looked around as Quinn and Jake maneuvered through bodies to reach them. "Well? Who's the bet taker, anyway?"

Hawk cleared his throat. "Well, ah…"

Oh no he hadn't. Melanie laughed. "How in the world are you the bet taker? You've been all over the world lately."

Mrs. Joskly, the librarian, handed Hawk an envelope. "He had help. I mean, since I was here."

"And since I gave ten percent to the library," Hawk said with a grin.

Melanie slipped her arms around Colton's waist. "I'm thinking a June wedding."

He grinned and kissed her again. "You name the date, and I'll be there. In fact, maybe I'll even sing as you walk down the aisle."

The crowd erupted into a series of "Hell no" and groans around them.

Melanie kissed him back. "I love you."

"I love you, too, Mel. Always." He kissed her again.

Epilogue

Melanie stood on the raised dais, sucking in her stomach. The wedding dress fit perfectly, but she had to quit eating such large breakfasts. Ever since Colton had moved in with her a day after her proposal, she'd been eating whatever he cooked.

Dawn stood on the next dais, her blue bridesmaid gown perfectly matching her stunning eyes. "You have not gained weight."

"Maybe not yet, but I can't keep eating like that. Your brother eats like a horse." Melanie held still as the seamstress tucked pins in along the bodice.

"They all do. Remember them as teenagers? The food was always gone before I could get to the pantry." Dawn gave a mock shrug. "So, have you seen the guys in their tuxes yet?" She kept her gaze on her sparkly shoes.

"Not yet. But I bet Hawk looks amazing," Melanie said. The guys were trying on tuxes on the other side of the wall, their boisterous laughter echoing through.

Dawn looked up. "I know, right?"

"Yeah. Did you ask him to your graduation?" Melanie asked.

Dawn shrugged. "Yes, but he didn't confirm. Graduation is in a month, and I know he'll just be getting the gyms started."

"If construction goes as planned." Melanie eyed the snow billowing around outside the window of the Mineral Lake dressmaker. "We just broke ground last week."

She couldn't believe she'd been engaged for almost a month. The wedding was planned for the end of June and she couldn't wait. But she'd wanted everything to be perfect, and perfect took time.

Dawn stepped down. "I'm glad you guys are going to live in your house, I've always loved your place."

"Me too." Melanie's stomach growled. While Colton had planned on building a house on his family's property, he was more than happy to live in hers…while they combined the ranches into an even larger land holding.

Heat climbed up her back, and she breathed deep. "I think the bodice is too tight."

The seamstress tugged on the fabric. "No, I think it's fitting perfectly."

Melanie's head spun. "Um, I don't feel so well."

Dawn glanced up. "Oh, no. The flu is really going around. The elementary school even closed early yesterday, my mom said. Are you hot?"

"Yes." Melanie swayed on the dais. Her knees weakened, and she went down.

"Mel!" Dawn yelled and hustled forward, bending down. "What's going on?"

"I don't know." Melanie rolled over and shoved to her knees. "My head is spinning."

"Melanie?" Colton called from the other section of the store. "Are you all right? Dawn? What's going on?" A rustling echoed, and the door started to open.

"Don't come in," Melanie gasped, shoving down bile.

"He can't see you in the dress," the seamstress hissed.

Melanie's head lolled, and she dropped all the way down.

"Colton?" Dawn called. "Hurry."

A door banged open, and strong arms cradled her. Colt's strong scent of leather and man surrounded her, offering comfort.

Her stomach lurched. "Oh, God."

The room spun as she was lifted and carried into the cold air. "You can't see my dress," she moaned.

"I didn't look." He hurried down the sidewalk.

A door opened, and warmth brushed her cheeks. She shut her eyes and rested against his chest, his heartbeat grounding her. "I think I have the flu."

The lone nurse in the small clinic instructed Colton to take her to a back examination room, where Doc Mooncaller loped in, his hair braided down his back. "Hi, Mel. The flu's going around. Have you vomited?" He reached out and felt her forehead. "You're not hot."

"Yes, she is," Colt quipped.

Doc laughed, his belly shaking. "Funny. Okay, let's check you out, darlin'. Do you want him to leave?"

"No," Colton said.

Melanie shrugged. "I don't care. If I have the flu, he's probably next."

"Hmmm." Doc felt her neck. "Let's see what's up."

During the next hour, he tested her, she peed in a cup, and she finally settled back on the examination table to wait.

"I hate the flu," she moaned, her arm over her eyes.

"Me too." Papers rustled as Colton kept reading through a magazine on fishing. "Your dress is stunning, by the way."

She groaned. Now she'd have to find a different dress. There was no way she was beginning her marriage with bad luck. "Everything is planned and has to be perfect. I'll get another dress."

Doc cleared his throat.

Melanie sat up. She hadn't heard him enter.

He rubbed his chin. "So, about perfect and planning."

She frowned. "Yes?"

"Ah, you're pregnant."

The world screeched to a stop. Her body shuddered. Tears slammed into her eyes. "No, I'm not." She glanced at Colton, whose intense gaze was checking out her abdomen. "I'm not," she said weakly, afraid to believe.

Doc glanced down at the chart in his hands. "Oh, you definitely are with child." He eyed Colton and then her. "Um, is this okay?"

Colton shot to his feet. "Oh, yeah!" He grabbed her and spun her around.

Her stomach revolted, and she slapped a hand against his chest. "Stop."

"Oh." He tucked her close. "Sorry."

She lifted her head, not caring tears slid down her face. "A baby."

Colton nodded, his eyes wet. "Yeah. A baby."

Melanie reached for him, needing his strength. Colton had always been there for her, always loved her. Now he'd love their baby just as strongly.

She looked back and grinned, her heart on fire for him. "I love you."

Acknowledgments

There are so many folks who help to make sure a book becomes a final product—many behind the scenes.

Thanks to my husband, Tony, because you're the best! Thanks to Gabe and Karly—I'm so proud of both of you!

Thank you to my wonderful agent, Caitlin Blasdell—as well to the gang at Liza Dawson Associates—you're a wonderful group.

Thank you to my editor, Liz Pelletier, whose edits make me laugh while we make the book stronger. Thanks also to Heather Howland for the awesome covers, and to my entire Entangled team.

Thanks also to my hardworking Facebook Street Team—you're a lot of fun, and you always make me smile. I appreciate the hard work.

Finally, thank you to my constant support system: The Englishes, Smiths, Wests, Zanettis, Chapmans, and Namsons.

About the Author

New York Times bestselling author Rebecca Zanetti has worked as an art curator, Senate aide, lawyer, college professor, and a hearing examiner—only to culminate it all in stories about Alpha males and the women who claim them. She writes contemporary romances, dark paranormal romances, and romantic suspense novels.

Growing up amid the glorious backdrops and winter wonderlands of the Pacific Northwest has given Rebecca fantastic scenery and adventures to weave into her stories. She resides in the wild north with her husband, children, and extended family who inspire her every day—or at the very least give her plenty of characters to write about.

Visit Rebecca at:
www.rebeccazanetti.com
www.facebook.com/RebeccaZanetti.Author

Discover Rebecca Zanetti's
Maverick Montana *series...*

AGAINST THE WALL

The last thing Sophie Smith expects when surveying land for her new golf course is to be yanked atop a stallion by a cowboy. And not just any cowboy—Jake Lodge, the Tribal lawyer opposing her company's development. But Sophie has banked everything on the golf course's success. She can't fail, no matter how tempting Jake may be.

UNDER THE COVERS

Juliet Montgomery fled to Montana to escape her not-so-law-abiding family, but when someone back home finds her in the small town near the Kooskia reserve, sexy sheriff Quinn Lodge must push aside his own demons—and try to contain his explosive attraction to Juliet—to keep her safe.

Printed in Great Britain
by Amazon